Promises of Yesteryears

Shadows of the past, Echoes of the future

Praveen Koval

StoryBeatz

StoryBeatz

StoryBeatz

An imprint of StoryBeatz LLC

story-beatz.com

To **Usha**: Happiness is being married to your best friend. I love you for always bringing the best out of me and keeping me inspired.

To **Adi** and **Arya**: To remind me, age is not something that matters. And for bringing out that little kid in me.

To my **Dad**: I know you are always watching over me from heaven.

To my **Mom**: The first person to show me how to hold a pencil and write.

To my brothers **Prashanth** and **Naveen**: For all the childhood memories, the movies we watched, and the cricket matches we played together.

To my cousin brother **Sivaprasad**: For making me realize there is an artist in me.

Chapter 1

Megan

♥

Anniversary Day: Monday

If love could be represented with musical notes, mine would be a symphony. If love were water droplets, mine for you would fill the Pacific. Here's to the celebration of love, genuine, not phony. It's been seven years with you, and it has been– what rhymes with Pacific, now– *beatific.*

I smiled at the note I was writing Kevin, my husband. I would slip it into his pocket at the anniversary dinner later tonight. I woke up this morning feeling what I could only describe as joy– joy at being so blessed by the universe to have such a thoughtful and loving husband as Kevin.

He was ever so sensitive to my needs, very supportive, and understanding. His smile could light up a bleak room like it lit up my otherwise mundane life. Before I met him, my love life was practically defunct, but I met him, and everything changed.

I looked up from the dusty pink card that I had drenched in the vanilla-lavender perfume he told me he loved so much. My reflection in the mirror stared right back at me, those azure eyes bright with life. If I had a dollar for each time, I was told I looked like a model or for each time random ladies asked for my skincare routine because 'I was literally glowing,' I'd have been lending the World Bank money. It was hard not to look so radiant when Kevin took such good care of me. That, and great genes.

I wasn't always this confident or secure about my looks until he popped on the scene. It felt like my life had suddenly become a fairytale, and I had just met my prince.

A glance at the well-tucked side of the king-sized bed told me Kevin had gotten up early. I must have been very deeply asleep, unaware of when he woke up and left for work. He must not have kissed my head before leaving. I've had to remind him, too, of late.

'It's probably just forgetfulness... it's okay,' I thought, as I righted the bottles he must have upset in his hurry. My wrist was tickled by the clear bristles of the hand-crafted hair brush we got on our last visit to Bali. I picked it up, memories of that sunny weekend flooding my mind. We separated at some point during the tour to get each other the best souvenir within a fifteen-minute frame.

A chuckle escaped my lips on remembering how I ran through the souvenir stalls at the rather-crowded market, hoping to find something that would catch my eye and fit into my budget.

They must have thought me crazy, with my jet-black curls bouncing about me 'untamed'.

The dresser was filled with adorable bits and pieces from our not-so-many travels. You could say we were a bit sentimental, and you wouldn't be wrong.

Or maybe I was the sentimental one. That being said, I have planned an anniversary party for Kevin and me. He doesn't know, of course. It's the least I could do to celebrate him after seven years of us braving countless storms together.

He deserves nothing but the best this world had to offer, and I'd give him that– as much as my capacity would allow.

Working remotely as a writer and editor for one of New York's magazines certainly did have its benefits. It gave me a flexible schedule and a decent income, at least. I've been saving up for this surprise party since our last anniversary. Our previous anniversary was a bit dull because we had to cancel plans due to him suddenly needing to work overtime that day. He sure doesn't get enough credit– he's such a hard worker.

So, this year, I thought about how to make this seventh anniversary different. Traditionally, the gifts should be copper and wool, so I got us matching copper bracelets with the nicknames we gave each other engraved on the inner side– he was 'Starlight,' mine was 'Sparkle.' I just can't wait to see his expression once he sees them. I also had matching ponchos woven for us. Grey, of course. Kevin rarely wore any other color in winter.

There, I had the gifts out of the way. Now, on to the surprise party planning. It was scheduled for 7:00 pm later tonight, and I haven't heard from the caterers or even Shanice, who promised to help with the decorations. It occurred to me that the drinks have to be bought and iced. I need my hair cut and my nails done. There was so much to be done, and I hadn't even started the day's activities.

At noon, I sat in the hairdresser's chair, leafing through her catalog of styles absentmindedly.

"Have you decided on a style yet?" the cheery lady asked, clasping her hands in front of her.

Of course, I had decided on a style beforehand. I was going to get a blowout. Kevin loves when my curls become loose waves with curtain bangs that frame my face. I wasn't really big on using heat on my hair, but since Kevin loves it, it couldn't kill me to style my hair like that every once in a while. Not to mention, it could be rather expensive getting my full head of luscious curls to lay flat. Today, I wouldn't mind splurging on my hair– the occasion called for it.

My nail appointment was at three, and I just had to hope the dresser would be done by then. *How I hate being late!*

While I sat under the dryer, I used the opportunity to text Shanice to remind the girls to turn up at the stroke of seven. They've been practically sisters to me since we moved to the Tri-state area. *Sunny Shanice, Tough Tori, Amazing Andrea, and Cheeky Candace.*

That's how I saved their numbers on my phone, and truth be told, those adjectives aptly summed up their personalities. There was more to them, of course, but... you get the gist. Of the four, I was closest to Shanice.

Their husbands hung out with Kevin also. I think we've been on two, three trips together, the ten of us if my memory serves me right. It seems only logical to have them around on such an important day to us. In fact, the surprise anniversary party was partly their idea.

I was good to go for my nail appointment before three, and I couldn't be more glad I was on time. I was still torn between getting a classic french manicure set or a nude almond-shaped set. *What would Kevin like?* The answer came almost immediately. *Blood red stiletto nails.*

I sighed. Red wasn't a color I'd usually wear on my nails, but I'd make this compromise just this once.

"I'd like medium-length stiletto nails," I told the gum-chewing technician who had begun prepping my nails.

Without taking her eyes off my nails, she asked, "What color?"

Then I had an idea. *Why not mix Kevin's and I's preferences?*

"I'd like a nude and red ombre."

She nodded in response before muttering something along the lines of, "A woman of culture."

I smiled, glad even the technician approved of my style choice. Two quick stops had to be made before it was seven, and I was running out of time. I wanted to have still enough time to get ready before everyone showed up.

The florist didn't waste my time at all. As I walked into her shop, some of my bustling feelings dampened a bit. There is a thing about the smell of fresh flowers that I find rather relaxing, so yeah, I patronize her quite a bit.

I got a small pot of white roses to match our room's decor and to give the room a different look, at least.

My last stop was at Kate's Confectionery. The gilded cake with whipped cream that I ordered was beautiful to look at. She must have really spent her time crafting the seven tiny gold quavers I had requested to be put by the side– I only hope Kevin actually sees them and notice. Each quaver stood for a year that we've been together.

In the taxi that took me home, all I was thinking about was how this party would turn out. It took all my self-restraint not to giggle in the car.

I didn't invite a lot of people as I had planned for it to be a small gathering– just friends and some neighbors. Kevin's sister was supposed to be present, but she had some engagements down in Iowa, so she couldn't make it to our anniversary party.

The red satin dress I picked out for tonight had hung in my closet for some days. I put it on and donned an oversized bathrobe over it. I contemplated eating something but knew I was too excited to keep my food down. I'd probably just eat after the party; at least, then, the jitters would be gone.

It was almost 6:30 when I heard the elevator bell ring in the hallway. I tried to look normal. 'Act normal,' I chided myself and hurried to the door to help relieve him of his bike. That bike sure had saved us a lot of cash in commute. He leaned against the doorframe, visibly exhausted, as I enveloped him in a hug. The familiar, comforting scent of sandalwood, pine, and his fresh sweat hit my nostrils, and I just wanted to burrow into him and stay there.

"Darling! Happy Wedding Anniversary!"

His hands slowly crept around my waist, hugging me back. It's been seven years, but his touch still makes my body tingle each time. I guess it's like that when you're in love with someone.

"Happy anniversary, babe. I had to leave early this morning to meet with a client. Hope you didn't miss me too much?"

"How wouldn't I?"

I pouted, feigning annoyance. My head was at his chest, so I knew I must look silly looking away like that. I tilted my head to look at him; his jaw taut and sharp, those lips of his ever luscious, ever tempting...

Without thinking further, I tiptoed and pressed my lips against his. His lips parted ever so slightly, tasting chocolate and something else I could not quite place. *Maybe he grabbed a snack on his way back.* 'Poor baby, he must be so hungry,' I thought as I shepherded him towards our room.

"So, tonight being our anniversary night, I have something little planned out, but first, I'd need you to take a shower and get dressed."

He glanced sideways at me, his expression hard to read, so I quickly added, "Or would you rather eat something first?"

"No, I'm not that hungry. I ate something before coming."

Just then, Candace's call came in. I tried to be as vague as possible on the phone, but Kevin's smart. He probably already picked up on a thing or two.

I noticed he was having a bit of a problem getting his blazer off, so I helped ease it off his back before proceeding to undo the buttons of his white shirt. His tie was off already and stuffed in his trouser pocket.

I ran my newly-done nails up and down his chest, teasing him as I slowly unbuttoned the shirt that had hugged his 42-inch chest all day long. *What wouldn't I have given to be that shirt?* Not me fangirling over my husband till now. I chuckled.

He seemed rather impatient to get out of the shirt and didn't even notice my manicure. 'It must be the exhaustion,' I thought as I watched him kick off his pants and leave them on the ground instead of dropping them in the laundry basket. Candace's call was a short one, and I was grateful for it.

"Littering still, pretty boy?" I said as I heard the faucet turn on, and though I knew he couldn't listen to me, I continued still. "I think you should start paying me to pick up after you since you're too big to do it yourself, Star...."

My words dried up in my mouth as I saw what fell out of his pocket when I shook it. I felt my world spin at such a dizzying speed and crash around my ears with a loud bang.

The headache that came on was immediate, and it felt like all the air had been sucked out of me.

I expected just his tie to fall out so I could put his clothes in their respective color sections, but I was in for a terrible, terrible surprise.

Two blue polythene squares fell out as well, and I first thought my brain was playing tricks on me, but there they lay, their outlines harsh against the immaculate white of the marble floor. One torn and empty, the other intact.

Condoms.

Was Kevin seeing another woman? And no, it couldn't have been bought for us because I'm allergic to latex. I mean severe allergies, complete with anaphylactic shock.

Well, I didn't think I'd be experiencing another type of shock on handling latex. The shock that the love of my life had been gracing other women's beds, touching them, kissing them, pleasuring...

I shuddered just thinking about it. I wasn't sure my legs could still bear my weight properly, so I went to sit on the bed, my gaze never leaving those treacherous blue squares that lay on my bedroom floor.

He got out of the shower five minutes later, dripping wet with just a tiny towel wrapped around his waist. On a typical day, looking at him like that while trying to say something serious would have distracted me. His auburn hair was now a wet chestnut, and the curls on his chest were adorable. The light sprinkling of hair on his lower torso, narrowing as it went along, like an arrow pointing to treasure, would have been enough to throw me off course on any other day, but not today.

I looked at him, finding disgust perched where admiration once used to be.

"What are those, Kevin?" I calmly asked, gesturing at the blue nylons on the floor with my pedicured foot. Funny how when I was getting my pedicure done, I didn't think it would be later used to point out evidence of my husband cheating. Ironic, isn't it?

His eyes followed my feet's direction and landed on the condoms on the floor. His face was, at first, a mixture of shock and alarm, and then it cooled down to just plain indifference.

After what felt like an eternity, he spoke. He didn't even try to deny it. He sighed and said, "I didn't want you to find out this way."

It sounded to me like a stranger had uttered those words. I couldn't believe my ears.

"How did you want me to find out, Kevin?" I asked, even as I felt my fragile, calm composure cracking.

"Well, for one, certainly not on our anniversary," Kevin grunted, heading to his drawer to pick out briefs.

Tears, like needles, pricked my eyeballs, threatening to flood their way through. My restraint was at its peak, but I still managed to squeak out, "Who's she?"

Not like I really wanted to know the nitty-gritty of their affair, but I needed my brain to realize the other woman was a real, living, breathing person and my husband was long gone without me even realizing.

"Well, Kelly..."

"I'm Megan, goddammit!"

He held out his hands placatingly. "No, no. I mean, her name is Kelly. She works in the same building as I...uh, I've been seeing her for about six months now...."

"Six months? That's all it took for you to throw our seven years into the trash? We've been married for seven years, Kevin! Seven years!" I screamed at him, livid at the nonchalant manner he addressed me. I think I saw him flinch as a result.

Well, he had better flinch. I rarely raised my voice. I rarely got mad. But this. This was unacceptable!

"I'm just not happy, Meg," he said, unable to meet my eyes. He stared at the ceiling in what looked to me like the joy of liberation, then added, "I actually haven't been for a long time. And I know that you are, and it kills me to ruin that for you, but if we end it now, maybe we can both move on to bigger and better things."

Bigger and better things. The nerve. The effrontery!

He looked at me like a lost puppy and tried to take my shaking hands in his. Once upon a time, that would have been a comforting gesture, but now it was just plain repulsive. I snatched my hands away, my eyes blazing in anger.

You know, I tried really hard to be the perfect wife. I was sacrificing over and again without thinking twice for the sake of his happiness and his career. A career that, evidently, led him right into the arms of another woman. Just how cruel could life be?

"So you want a divorce?" I ask, somewhat hoping he'd decline and maybe, just maybe, we could work on our issues and move past this.

But the look on Kevin's face hinted otherwise. He looked sheepish but seemed to glow with glee.

"Yes."

Yes. Never had a monosyllabic word ever sounded so long and heavy in my ears. The same *yes* that I said to a happily ever after was now the word that ushered me into my misery.

Maybe it was the hurt in my eyes or just pity for the helpless woman that stood before him, and he went on to say things along the lines of, "...we can still be a part of each other's lives... maybe even bring each other to family functions. We don't have to be enemies or anything. What do you think?"

I didn't reply to him. He probably mistook my silence for consent cause he went even further to say, "I really think you and Kelly would get along nicely...you know, maybe once the anger fades and you're more... logical?"

Did he just insult me? I looked at him like he was frothing at the mouth. Raving mad.

I pushed past him to get to the bathroom cabinet. I had to prepare my face for tonight's event. I had planned a party after all, and since it was too late to cancel, I might as well just look good. It didn't take me long, either. I slapped on some nude lipstick and highlighted my cheekbones and the bridge of my nose. Nothing over the top. I already feel stupid enough to wear such a pretty dress at my anniversary-turned-divorce party.

I dropped the brush, willing myself not to cry as I stepped out of the bathroom to a fully-dressed Kevin.

He looked like he was going to say something, but then the doorbell rang, cutting him short.

"Looks like our guests are here already. Silly me that planned an anniversary party."

In ten minutes, the place was in full swing. Tori had come with a music box, and some of our favorite songs were reeling out.

Kevin had the guts to show up at the living room entrance, looking all surprised. I nearly puked in my cocktail at his effortless pretense. It made me wonder *how long he had been pretending with me.*

Andrea moderated the event, giving slots to four people to say what they loved about us.

Shanice's hand shot up first. Then Dave Heaton, then Henrietta, his wife, and Tori. Tori, who never spoke publicly, wanted to talk at my anniversary! If only it were worth it.

The nice words and actions made my head hurt even though I kept a smile on throughout. Kevin still played the role of the perfect husband, making me sick to my stomach, and I couldn't have been happier than when Shanice left after helping me clean up a bit. She noticed something was off, but I couldn't bring myself to talk about it just yet.

The lies. The hurt. The pretense. The cheating. So much that it washed away the joys of the past. The joys and the promises of yesteryears.

Chapter 2

Kevin

♥

Anniversary Day: Monday

It was my wedding anniversary, but I wasn't... feeling anything. I knew Megan would be ecstatic and making plans to celebrate. It was our 7th, but it felt longer. I was starting to feel the strains of my pretense and going through the motions every day. Forcing myself to smile as she kissed me, looking into her eyes and recoiling because they didn't have that sizzling effect anymore.

I wondered what would be her present to me this year. Last year, it wasn't so bad as I knew I wanted to go but didn't have a destination yet. But Kelly fixed me. It made me whole again, in a way that Megan couldn't. I thought about what she would be doing at home, preparing for my arrival. I wondered what her gift to me would be. We celebrated everything. From Easter to birthdays and even the day we met. She was full of sunshine, but I wasn't reflecting anymore.

I was still hanging on to hope that she didn't plan anything. Maybe something simple, and I could get through today again. But as I came in and saw her bustling around the house, I knew another anniversary dinner was in the offing. She greeted me enthusiastically. Throwing herself at me, I smelt the lavender in her hair. The same fragrance I loved so much all those years ago.

I still remember our first anniversary. The anniversary of our marriage. There was no dinner and no guests. It was just the two of us at our apartment, and we decided to take a walk around the neighborhood. It was serene, and it was autumn. We hardly said anything, just strolling around in comfortable silence. I circled the block thrice and then came back in. It was simple. It was nice. It was love. But not anymore.

But now, I didn't know if I loved her anymore. I had to go through with the party or whatever dinner she had planned. I was already exhausted. I decide to take a bath, trying to steel myself for the ordeal.

She seemed happy. I knew I had been absent-minded lately. Our bedroom was as impeccable as ever. I could see the newly gotten roses she bought, near our bedpost, on the table next to our wedding pictures. I could also hear as she confirmed with the Heatons that they were coming to dinner too. Dave Heaton was a serial cheat, even though his wife always forgave him.

We were close once, but Megan dissuaded me from keeping his company. She didn't want his attitude to rub off on me. I smiled. He didn't do anything of such, and I knew for a fact that he still cheated on his wife. I had promised myself that I wouldn't be like those men that cheated on their partners with every chance they got.

I looked at myself in the mirror. Kevin Stewart. With my Italian suit and the gold cufflinks. I didn't look like other men my age. I looked younger, a lot younger. Megan had told me that many times as she stroked my hair on nights when we couldn't sleep.

She was talking to Candace now. She was already on her way and would arrive in an hour. Megan came over and helped remove my clothes as she ran her hand over my torso.

I hurried into the bathroom, putting my clothes in a heap near the bed. Megan would complain, but she would help with it. She always did; she would complain about my dirty habits just as she picked them up and put them with the laundry.

I stood in the shower, with the streams of water beating my back and the top of my head. I increased the temperature and waited as steam started to fill up the bathroom. It stung, and it was starting to hurt, but I stayed there. I could hear Megan's voice in the bedroom, and she must have been talking about my clothes, maybe because our life was boring and predictable. That wasn't it. We had fun, vacations, and dates once in a while, whenever we could break free from our schedules. But maybe that was it too. We had fun...

Megan was silent. I expected her to rave more. She hated it when I littered. Sometimes, I did it to annoy her. She looked beautiful when she was trying to get her point across forcefully. Then, she would burst out laughing before she issued a less stern warning. I stepped out, waiting for the usual barrage. But her back was to me, her head bent. She was standing over my clothes, and she was staring at something in her grasp.

"Meg?"

Then, she turned to me. Her eyes flashed, shining bright. There were tears. She was crying. Why...

And then I saw it. It was hard to notice it immediately. Her nails were recently done, and I had seen them but didn't give her compliments. I had been going through the motions lately and had made sure I ticked every box as I pretended to be myself. I was starting to slip recently, but the biggest of them all was in her hand. The condom I forgot to put back in my locker back at the gym. I thought I did. I joined the gym to have an excuse to spend more time with Kelly, as our work could sometimes be stifling. So, we met there, and I made sure I always had a stash of condoms in my locker, rarely taking them out.

Damn.

Maybe I was waiting for it to happen subconsciously. Perhaps I wanted it to happen. But not today, I saw her, and my heart broke. There was another feeling of relief that numbed that pain until I couldn't feel it anymore.

I wasn't going to deny it. It was bound to happen sooner rather than later.

"I didn't want you to find out that way."

The tears began to fall, rivulets, then fast-flowing streams. I felt evil. Megan was a sweet soul, always cheerful and in love. And I broke her heart. But there was nothing I could do. I felt remorse but not as much as I should have. Mostly, I just wanted it to be over.

"I didn't want you to find out this way."

I tried to soothe her, but she wasn't going to.

"How did you want me to find out, Kevin?"

I didn't have an answer to that. I had been putting this off for a while.

"Well, not on our anniversary, for one thing."

She was composed now. I could hear them catching in her throat as she struggled to keep them back. The sounds were like a dagger to my heart. I shouldn't have been able to stand it. But my heart was hardened. I didn't want it to happen this way, but I was prepared for any eventuality.

"Who is she?"

She asked suddenly.

"Well, Kelly..."

"I'm Megan, goddammit!"

She almost screamed. I felt she was going to start hitting me.

"No, no. I mean, her name is Kelly. She works in the same building as I...uh, I've been seeing her for about six months now...."

I sounded incoherent, unsure.

"Six months? That's all it took for you to throw our seven years into the trash? We've been married for seven years, Kevin! Seven years!"

She was screaming now. Her face contorted with anger and sorrow. I backed away. Her onslaught was starting to get to me. It was almost seven. Guests were going to start arriving very soon. But this had to be done.

Better now than never.

I went broke and told her the truth that I'd been holding back for a long time.

"I'm just not happy, Meg," I said

I looked at the ceiling. I couldn't deny the relief I was feeling.

"I actually haven't been for a long time. And I know that you are, and it kills me to ruin that for you, but if we end it now, maybe, we can move on to bigger and better things."

Beneath all the guilt I felt for betraying her, beneath the sadness I felt for making her feel this way, I felt relief. A breath of fresh air in a stuffed room. I tried to hold her hands and reassure her. Then I saw it, the anger and disgust in her eyes. I knew how much she hated cheating. She had been faithful, and I repaid her with the exact opposite.

"So you want a divorce?"

There was hope in her voice. She thought we could move on, like the Heatons. But I was going to have to crush it. There was no time for half-measures. I was ripping the Band-Aid off her fresh wound. It was going to be excruciating, but this had to be done again.

"Yes."

As I replied, I wondered how awkward the anniversary dinner was going to be. If suppose it was going to be held at all. She was silent. I decided to use this opportunity.

"This isn't the end. We can still be a part of each other's lives... maybe even bring each other to family functions. We don't have to be enemies or anything. What do you think?"

She remained quiet.

"I really think you and Kelly would get along nicely...you know, maybe once the anger fades and you're more... logical?"

Her face flushed. I saw the anger in her eyes. I had pushed it too far. She shoved me aside and walked away. I was still standing, almost naked, in the center of the room. The condoms she had found were on the ground next to my clothes.

I wondered if she would want to go ahead with the party. I didn't care, and I was just glad it was over. Kelly had been pushing me to ask for a divorce, and I had been evading her requests. But now I didn't have to do anything. It was over just as soon as it began. There was an extra spring in my step as I gathered my suit and trousers in my hands and moved to the laundry bag.

I was going to call Kelly and invite her to dinner. Usually, she never called or texted me once I got home. It was an unspoken rule. She would be shocked that I broke that custom.

But she came back into the room looking freshened. Before I could say anything, the doorbell rang.

"Looks like our guests are here already. Silly me that planned an anniversary party."

I looked at her in disbelief. Indeed, she wasn't going ahead with the party. But she was. Apparently, it was going to be torture. She stepped out and welcomed her friends one after the other as they brought gifts. I made sure I kept up appearances. I was faking smiles and conversations that I didn't want to have. Finally, it was over.

After they left, she was surprisingly civil, speaking as few words as possible and avoiding me at every turn. I didn't force her, didn't want to push her, but I wanted to tell her what I had decided some time ago. She slept beside me, not saying a word. Stayed as far away from me as possible, near the edge of the bed. I was hurt in a way, I didn't want her to see me as repulsive, but there was nothing I could do about that. And I felt what I would tell her in the morning would be even less palatable than her discovery today.

Chapter 3

Kevin

♥

Day Zero: Tuesday

I woke up and went to get her coffee. Hopefully, she was calm after the previous night. She wasn't in her bed. I looked at the space we shared for many nights. The bed and sheets we used to roll on changed a few times over the years, but the foundation remained solid. Not anymore.

I walked up to her. She was staring out the window on the balcony, looking down at the neighbors. She came here when she wanted to think about her books when she hit a block and wanted some inspiration. This was where I wanted to talk to her about a divorce. I felt like I was desecrating every part of her life.

"Megan, I don't know if you've guessed this already. But... I want a divorce."

She didn't move, and there was no indication that she'd heard me. I touched her, running my index finger on the outside of her elbow. There was no flinch this time.

"Okay. I understand."

There were tears in her eyes again.

"I'll agree to it. You don't have to add agreements. Just bring it, and I'll sign."

She was sad, her heart was broken, and I was the cause. The tears in her eyes, her trembling upper lip, and even the wind that blew her hair into her face, making them wet with her tears, all seemed to contribute to her bravado and grit, her refusing to beg and grovel for a second chance.

I had imagined this happening a lot of times, but this was not one of the possible outcomes I had envisaged. I expected her to be enraged and vow never to agree.

"Thank you very much, and I had thought you would...."

She waved her hand quickly, cutting me off.

"There is one condition, Kevin. I have some requests that I would like you to...."

It was my turn to cut her off. It was then I saw the anger in her eyes. She had been hiding it well.

" What do you want?"

"Time. Your time. Just two weeks."

I was confused. There was a slight smile on her face.

"We have spent seven years together. I think two weeks is the least you can give me since you're eager to leave."

When she put it that way, it was hard to refuse.

"So, you want me to stay for two weeks? Just that, and you'll sign it?"

I wanted to be sure. She smiled again, but there was only sadness on her upturned lips.

"Yes, Kev. But you would do something for me every day. A single request. Then, I will sign whatever you want."

Megan pushed past me, leaving me with my thoughts. She was smart. Maybe I shouldn't have agreed so soon. I didn't know what she had in store for me. I prepared and left for the office. There was nothing she could do to stop me from leaving. I had made up my mind.

Chapter 4

Megan

♥

Day Zero: Tuesday

I endured the night I had looked forward to for a year. I grit my teeth and forced smiles, willing myself to go through with the party I had planned.

I don't know whether to be grateful I knew the truth at last or if I'd have preferred to live in my fairytale for a bit longer. Except that Kevin wasn't happy anymore, and the last thing I'd do is to keep him bound in a marriage he no longer wanted.

Throughout the evening, I played the perfect host, showering each person with compliments– they deserved it. It just hurt watching them shower him also with compliments, none of which he deserved. I heard words like *loving, faithful, admirable...* It made me laugh. Not a pleasant, mirthful laugh, of course.

He was an ungrateful, tactless little boy with a memory problem. No, because how dare he forget all I did...all we've been through together?

I did have a bit more margarita than I should have, but not even the alcohol could numb the pain or fill the gaping wound the reveal left in my chest.

Listening to everyone go on and on about the happy couple made me occasionally smile at Kevin as it was a pleasure watching him look slightly uncomfortable at first, then he slipped into his Oscar-winning actor self and even managed to look pleasantly surprised and awed at all the nice words.

To think he even gave a little speech about how lovely the party was, praising me for being a virtuous woman who stood by him and whatnot. I wondered for a second back there if he was going to announce our divorce.

I was so angry that I wouldn't have cared. Maybe I would have...even if it was just a little. It hurt so much.

Soon, everyone started leaving for their homes, and I could swear I heard Henrietta asking her husband why they hadn't hosted an anniversary party like the Stewarts.

I shuddered. The party wasn't bad, but I certainly don't wish anyone under these conditions.

It felt like I was dead while alive. A walking martyr of self-immolation.

Shanice had been eyeing me suspiciously since I abruptly left for the bathroom right in the middle of Tori's moving speech. She saw me downing quite a few shots of brandy in between, as well. It wasn't usual for me to drink that much, so naturally, she was concerned.

"Baby girl, is everything alright? You look a little winded."

"Hmm, I feel sick."

It wasn't exactly a lie. I did feel sick—a combination of a spike of alcohol in my bloodstream and Kevin's sewer behavior.

"You were a bit heavy on the booze earlier too. Is everything good?"

I forced a smile. "It sure is. Well, not really... but I'd tell you about it later."

"Alright. ...be good. And I hope you like the black lingerie I got you. It's naughty!"

I laughed at her last statement. But for a different reason than she thought. I was done making efforts for someone who had begun imagining life with another woman, and racy lingerie wasn't even on my list of priorities.

As I shut the door behind Shanice, I realize I'm finally alone. Alone with a stranger.

I hadn't even turned around when I heard his low baritone calling to me.

"Megan, can we talk?"

I swallowed the lump that was fast forming in my throat and blinked back the tears that made my vision blurry. I slowly turned around to face him.

Seeing his face was like a punch to my gut.

He looked exasperated.

"You're crying still? Come on, let's talk about this like mature adults. People fall out of love every time; stop making this a bigger deal than it is," he said, throwing his hands up in frustration.

"How about you leave me alone, huh? I'm not ready to have this conversation with you. Maybe tomorrow, I will."

He sighed, shaking his head as though I was the problematic, unreasonable teenager throwing a tantrum.

"Honestly, quit being so difficult... how about we talk about this tomorrow?"

The tears threatened to fall, but I held them back with every resolve I had. Kevin would not get the satisfaction of seeing me break down and weep. *I can hold it in for a little longer, just a bit longer, till Kevin is gone.*

I let loose when I heard the door to the bedroom we once shared shut. I let the tears flow with reckless abandon; they were the only testament to the pain that raged in my veins.

Like a small shrub in a hurricane, I felt uprooted entirely– without respite or shade.

I tossed and turned on the bed in the guest room, unable to whip up the strength or willpower to go to my former bedroom.

Yes, *former*. Just like how Kevin was about to become my ex-husband.

Wasn't I enough? Had I lost my allure without even realizing it? Was I guilty of something that pushed him to the hands of another woman?

Did I complain too much? Did I push him too hard?

So many questions swarmed my banging head, but there were no answers. I moved over to the window and stared down at the empty street. I sure did make a grave mistake letting us buy this house in his name. I'd have to move out of this neighborhood soon, too.

Watching the moonlight dance on the tarred road brought a wistful smile to my lips as memories came flooding in.

When we just moved in, we rented bikes and raced each other down the road like children, giggling and content with each other.

We came in later, tired, but we exhausted ourselves further by devouring each other on the kitchen countertop– our bedroom was too far away.

Or was it the dinner dates we had fortnightly? Was his sweetness in these past months a lie? Or did I mistake his civility for love? I must have been so blind for so long.

I considered drenching my taste buds in ice cream as if numbing my tongue would numb the throbbing ache in my heart. Yet, I got out of bed and headed for the fridge. The painting of the sea goddess he bought because he said it reminded him of me sat on the wall across from me as though taunting me.

The roiling waves around her were riddled with music symbols– a glorified Siren. I think I know why he said it reminded him of me now. It's a pity, he now probably finds Kelly's sounds more appealing to his ears.

He had me in that sultry pose many times, my back arched in the throes of pleasure, while he worshipped me– his Sparkly Goddess.

I shook my head, trying to rid myself of the thought. It was so weird that what once gave me pleasure was now a source of unimaginable sorrow to me.

My steps were as heavy as my heart, each slower than the last. Eventually, I got to the fridge, where we used to tape love notes to each other. He stopped writing back, blaming his busy schedule.

How could I have missed this sign? How far back had he fallen out of love with me?

How could I have been too self-absorbed to notice?

My head lolled on its own accord and leaned against the door of the fridge. My knees grew weak with the realization that I had kept a man in a loveless, one-sided marriage for so long, and my vanity didn't let me see past my nose.

Everywhere I turned in this house, memories of us assaulted me.

The large portrait of us on the wall didn't help either. We both wore white dress shirts and jeans, holding hands as we kicked the beach sand, our faces the image of mirth and young love.

It was taken on one of our visits to Coney Island beach. We went just to take pictures, and indeed, we took some of our best pictures that day. Looking at the picture, memories of the day popped up in my head with incredible detail– the bright sun overhead, the sharp feeling of the beach sand between my toes, the ice-cold popsicles we shared after, the bird poop that ruined the back of his white shirt– it made me laugh despite my shitty mood.

It was a lovely summer, and that was the season of life that we were in, and now, I could feel the slight chill of autumn creeping into my bones; his love for me dried up and withered like maple leaves in autumn. I chuckled a mirthless chuckle, wondering what the Fates were playing at, ushering me into Fall by letting the love of my life fall out of love with me.

The little laughter soon dulled from shame. Shame for being a delusional, insensitive wife. A negligent spouse, that's what I was.

Due to my negligence, I lost Kevin. It was no other's fault but mine. I pressed my left palm over my mouth to stifle the nerve-racking sobs that escaped my broken soul.

'But that couldn't be true,' I thought as I reached for a tub of mint chocolate ice cream. 'Everything I did, I did for him. Even at times when his family abandoned him somewhat, I remained by his side, nursing him back to health. No, I don't think I was self-absorbed.'

With that, I trudged back to my new room, ensuring I focused on my feet so as not to be distracted by the memories of us that littered the house. I only paused to swipe aspirin from the supplies kitchen cabinet– a massive hangover was to be expected, and I had to be ready.

Maybe I wasn't self-absorbed, but I focused on the wrong things, perhaps? Times when I burnt herself out with no more energy left to give– writing did take its toll on the mind and body. Maybe, those nights I turned him away because I was tired culminated in this.

I couldn't help but recollect moments I spent time focusing on friends and extended family needs because I felt Kevin and I were in a good place, and he was so understanding, and it did appear to me like they needed me more. I hope it was not that I took his softness and understanding for granted. Could it be that I neglected him while caring for others? I bit down on my lip hard. *Could this be why?*

I tried frantically to push the memories aside. They weren't so palatable, and if I wanted to save my marriage, I should probably focus my energy on looking forward and not reminiscing.

I sighed and shoved another spoonful of the green ice in my mouth, pacing in my room.

Then, like a thunderbolt, it hit me. There was something I could do after all.

And, do it, I shall.

Chapter 5

Kevin

♥

Day One: Wednesday

I woke up early, but she had already left for the gym. The events of the past couple of days went through my head. In a way, it was surreal knowing that I would be divorcing Megan. She didn't want to let go easily, but she had no choice.

There was a pink card lying conspicuously on the center table in the middle of the living room, right next to the flowers the Heatons got us for our anniversary. I picked it up, curious as to what it said.

> *1. Remember the gift I got you at that gift shop? That was the first gift I ever gave to you. You promised to get me one from that gift shop* **doh**. *Could you do that today?*

~ *Megan*

I grunted. I almost pitied her. She couldn't stop holding on to the past and accepting the fact that we were over. I remember the watch quite alright. It was a nice handmade watch with unique craftsmanship from the House of Horology, and I know it could not have been cheap. But since that was what she wanted, there was no harm in that. I passed by the shop on my way to work. It was by the bus stop.

Moreover, anything could be a gift so far I have got it from that shop. Why that shop? She could have said I could get her a gift too.

I didn't know if I should get it. What would Kelly think? Would she want me to? Megan and I had had some good times, and I would be the first to admit that she didn't deserve this. But it would be cruel to give her some sort of false hope regarding us. I was with Kelly now. On the other hand, it was the least I could do, considering all the time we spent together.

Yesterday, when I left for the office, I told Kelly about recent developments. She didn't seem as enthusiastic as I thought she would be. She had been badgering me about the divorce proceedings for a while now, and when it was finally happening, it looked as if she wasn't so eager anymore.

"What's on your mind? You don't seem as excited as I thought you'd be. Have you changed your mind?"

She shook her head vehemently.

"No, that's not it. That's not it at all."

I didn't understand what could have caused this, and I told her.

"It's Megan. I don't understand what she meant by her requests. Must you do it? She could be using it as some sort of ploy to get you guys back together."

She was scared. Kelly held my gaze and smiled. We were in my office, and she was sitting on the edge of the table. She had dark flowing hair like Megan, but that was where the similarities ended.

I wish I had met Kelly before Megan. I always felt important to Kelly, and I felt like she couldn't do without me. Megan wasn't like that, and she could get engrossed in her writing for such a long time. There were times when we wouldn't say more than two sentences in a whole day. Those times I ordered takeout for both of us, ate mine, and returned the following morning to meet hers exactly where I'd left it.

Kelly was always excited to see me. Maybe that was because we just fell in love and were in some sort of honeymoon phase, but hers felt different. The way I felt for her was different.

"That won't happen," I reassured her, "I'm not going to do anything I'm uncomfortable with."

She nodded, and that was it. There was no need for extra words of affirmation. She believed anything I said.

"So, good thing I sneaked the condoms into your pocket then."

I was wide-eyed for a moment, laughter finding its way from my stomach. I thought I had forgotten to place them back in my gym locker.

It was a strange feeling, her taking matters into her own hands. Would I have come around to asking for a divorce from Megan without any inciting event? Maybe I would have eventually, but she accelerated the process. She knew what I wanted and made it happen. That was another difference between them. Megan would have preferred letting things work out themselves.

She was probably trying to make me remember the story behind the gift she gave me. It was back when we were at college, and I had no idea she was in love with me.

We had gotten close pretty quickly, and I was already thinking about asking her out. I was nervous and kept thinking she would shoot me down. I didn't want to ruin our friendship; asking her on a date would make things awkward if she refused.

I was an intern when we first met. She was a student at Princeton University in New Jersey. Weeks after we met,

I told her I was preparing for an internship interview at another company with excellent pay.

Around the same time, some guys in my department were throwing a party. Megan had always been the more sensible one of the two of us, and when she told me not to go, I should have listened. But, I felt a chick I had just met should not be telling me what to do.

Deep down, I knew I should've stayed home and had a good night's rest in preparation for Monday, but I opted for the party.

The result was inevitable. I got drunk, got home, and slept my socks off. I had the nastiest hangover that Monday, and I had the interview still.

That morning, Megan called to say hi and wish me luck, heard how horrible I sounded, and magically appeared at my door with some sort of cocktail. I was up in a flash. I needed something to remind me not to be late. Even more, I knew I needed the stability only she could provide.

At work, I told Kelly about what Megan wanted.

"You don't have to get her anything. She has to sign the divorce papers. She can't force you to stay."

I shrugged.

"It's just a gift if you think about it. There's nothing more. I would prefer it if we signed the papers without any...mess."

Kelly is very vocal in her disagreement.

"She is trying to get in your head. Manipulate you. Don't you get it?"

"I know. But doesn't that negate the whole manipulation process?"

She almost screamed.

"Don't get her anything! Let her rave and rage. She can't tell you what to do."

She looked worried. Perhaps I was underestimating Megan.

"We have been together for seven years, and she didn't do anything to hurt me. I feel like I owe her this, at the very least."

Kelly rolled her eyes.

"You're so nice. You fell in love. She would be doing the same in your shoes. Think about that."

Then, she left my office.

She was angry that I was considering it in the first place. I texted her, assuring her I wouldn't. This would undoubtedly make Kelly happy, but I started to feel guilty. And as the day went on, I began to feel worse. There was a hole in my heart that was filled with guilt and some sort of pain.

Sure, there were many things about Megan that I wasn't going to miss. She snored a lot, and you would not have guessed from her posh exterior. It was something I never told her, together with the fact that she had bad taste in movies. Terrible taste. And she was a writer and supposed to have an excellent imagination. The movies she loved were bland and uninteresting. And she always wanted to wrangle every aspect of her life into submission. Everything had a natural order, and some problems would go away on their own, but it was as if she could never accept that.

But she had her good sides too. She was very thoughtful. The watch she got for me was what I had on. I wore it on Mondays and Wednesdays. She must have known I would wear it today and dropped that note. She was trying to manipulate me into feeling nostalgic.

I was taking the train home. The entrance to the subway tunnel was on the other side of the road, but as I was about to cross, I saw the gift shop right in front of me.

I was almost tempted to get something for Megan, but I heard Kelly's voice in my head, my assurance to her that I wouldn't get Megan anything. It was a battle of wills. Megan had been good to me for seven years. Whether I had fallen in love with another or not, I had wronged her. I could put myself in her shoes and knew how hurt she felt. I felt I should get her something. I knew I wouldn't budge no matter what happened, so no harm would be done if I decided to buy her a gift.

But what could I get her? I was at a loss. A couple of years ago, I would have had a headache choosing from a long list of possible Romantic choices. But now, I didn't know what to buy. I was out of touch with her for the past year. I had no idea what she would like anymore.

Then, I caught myself. Kelly was right. Without knowing it, I was already thinking of what to get Megan. Kelly was my future. I had to focus on her and nothing else. Megan would soon be my past. I wasn't getting her anything.

I walked across to the subway tunnel, not looking back.

No amount of gift-giving or note-writing would change my mind. I had to rip off the so-called band-aid once and for all. She was going to be hurt and heartbroken in the end. I was going to get the divorce I wanted, and that was it.

I met Megan in the living room, working on her PC. She didn't notice me immediately after I entered. She looked so serious, typing away at the keyboard. I cleared my throat, and she turned to face me. I didn't know what I expected. Maybe a civil greeting or something akin to that.

But she did neither. She kept staring at me.

After a while, it became uncomfortable.

"Where is it?"

I shrugged.

"Where is what?"

"I believe you saw my note?"

I hated the tone she used. She couldn't tell me what to do.

"I didn't get it. No amount of gifts is going to change anything, Megan. The earlier you realize this, the better."

Her face softened.

"Kevin, I made you dinner. Would you like to eat now, or would you want to freshen up first?"

I smirked.

"No. Don't bother. I ate already."

Her face fell, and I felt terrible. I turned around and went into the bedroom. I couldn't bear to see the look on her face. However, she followed me. I could see the tears in her eyes again.

"What did I do to you that was so wrong, huh?" she asks. "I know I'm not perfect, but I gave you everything I know how to give. How could you be with someone for seven years and not even care enough about them to pick up a silly little trinket on the way home from work?"

I had nothing today to say to that. She was correct. I was starting to see I was wrong. Or maybe I was feeling like that in the face of her tears. Kelly said other people's emotions too easily swayed me.

When she saw that she wouldn't get an answer, she walked out, but not before coming to take her sheets and pillow. She was going to the guest room to stay the night.

I considered going out to stay with Kelly. I didn't feel comfortable staying alone in our main bedroom, and I didn't want to leave Megan all alone in the house. I went to the guest bedroom to knock, but before I could, I heard her crying softly. The house was quiet, and I could hear her clearly through the door. My heart was hurting a little but hurting nonetheless.

I strengthened my resolve and left her to get over it.

I went to clear the dishes from the dining table. I had lost my appetite. I also did the dishes before retiring to the sofa.

I couldn't sleep. I couldn't toss and turn as the sofa was not comfortable. I looked around the house. Immediately, my eyes fell on our wedding pictures on the mantelpiece. We looked so happy. Who would have known that we would be trying to keep our marriage together seven years later? We had no kids and no joint accounts, and we liked it that way. Independent together, that was what we told each other.

Maybe we were too far apart and got farther as time passed, without realizing it until it was too late. I was fiercely protective of Megan. I didn't want any guy around her, and she loved my territorial attitude. My mind switched to when Megan told me she loved me. After the headaches I had, trying to figure out the right time to ask her out without it seeming awkward, she broke it to me softly when I finally gathered the courage.

I had thought about it for a while. Everyone thought we were dating, and we kept denying it. Up until I saw Denver getting closer. He asked her on many dates, and she agreed after much persuasion from her friends.

They went to a party. I didn't know why he would take her to a party as a date and why she would agree to go there with him in the first place. I thought she was finally gone from me. My mind was in great turmoil. I wasn't invited, but I could gain entry. I was contemplating crashing and telling Megan how I felt. I had already put on my shirt and was about to leave around midnight.

I looked disheveled, but I didn't think I was going to look out of place among those at the party. Then I heard a knock at my door. I didn't want to open it. It could be one of my friends looking for a study partner. But I wasn't in the mood, and they did want to know where I was going by midnight. But the knocking was persistent. Then, I heard my name. It was Megan.

"Hey, open up."

I didn't believe my luck. Running to the door, I opened it and almost dragged her in. For some reason, I thought she was in some sort of trouble.

"Meg. What happened? Did the police crash it?"

She laughed.

"No, they didn't. I just wanted to be somewhere else really bad."

Even then, it didn't occur to me. I have been told I could be thickheaded sometimes. But I think it mostly happened around Megan.

"Oh. Where did you want to be?"

She looked at me with a raised eyebrow, her face twisted as she tried to hold back her laughter. I still didn't get it. She gave up and sat on my bed, removing her shoes and earrings.

"I was coming to see you."

It was her turn to be confused.

"Why?"

I crossed my fingers behind me and told her everything. For a while, we were both silent. I could hear my heart pounding as she watched me through her intelligent eyes. When she told me how much she loved me, how much she waited for me to say to her, I didn't think I had felt such joy in all my days.

But it was all coming to an end. But she didn't deserve that. I was going to get her a gift tomorrow. No matter what.

Chapter 6

Megan

♥

Day One: Wednesday

The hollowness of my own heart resonated loudly in my ears. Never had I been able to relate to the term, *deafening silence* so much– just that, in my case, this house was not just silent but now empty. Devoid of passion, that burning ardor that we once had. The desire for each other that we had now lost.

I dragged myself up from the rumpled sheets, willing myself not to acknowledge what the tousled sheets reminded me of– nights of unbridled pleasure with award-winning crescendos.

There was no zeal in me to get out of bed, but I did anyway. I got up to prove to myself that I wasn't falling apart– yet. That, and the fact that I had three emergency articles to submit before the close of the day.

And there was the note I was going to write Kevin.

I had bought pink index cards for the private treasure hunt I wanted us to have in the weeks following our seventh anniversary, but... life sure had other, very bitter plans. The cards were in the room Kevin and I once shared, and I debated whether or not I had the strength or courage to go in there and retrieve them.

There were reams of paper I had stashed in the storage. I could use those instead. The storage in question was a refrigerator carton that I had managed to convert into a storage box, keeping stationery, memorabilia, and even handy tools. At that moment, though, it served as the toolbox for the construction project I had going on.

Project? That was laughable. It was almost like I was hinting that my actions would never have any effect. They never had, and there was still no indication that that trait would magically disappear anytime soon.

If I could influence anything so much, my marriage wouldn't be in chaos, and my world wouldn't be imploding on itself like it was.

The dust from the carton sent me wheezing, and I perched on the bed, eyeing the box suspiciously. I began to wonder if all this stress was even worth it; plus, what did I even think I could achieve by it anyway?

I pushed the negative thoughts out of my head and fished out a ream of paper and a pen. I sat cross-legged in front of the pen and paper, doubt eating into my resolve. After staring at it for what seemed to be an eternity, just sitting still and analyzing the cricket sounds outside, I picked up the pen, trying to trick myself into thinking I had gathered enough mental strength to compose the note I wanted to leave for Kevin.

If there were a plague I knew so easily beset writers such as myself, it would be the sudden loss of all writing-related cognitive reasoning when your self-expression is of utmost importance. That's the only reason why the best-selling author can run out of words to write to their spouse. I chuckled, shaking my head.

Writing came naturally to me, but at a time like this, when I desperately needed to convey my sincerest wishes, words were failing me. I scrunched up yet another sheet of paper after minutes of mindless doodling.

I decided to try again and pulled out another sheet from the pack. The blank off-white page stared back at me, daring me to sully it with black ink from my gel pen. I hissed and scrunched up the proud sheet, flinging the tight ball against the opposite wall.

It hit a tiny pink and white artwork of a quaint little cottage out in the countryside that hung on a wall, and I softened. I knew what I wanted to say, and I just needed to say it.

Broken promises, no matter how long ago, have to be redeemed somewhat, and half the time, that doesn't happen. I've made my fair share of promises and received more than my life's worth in promises as well, but if there was anything I absolutely abhorred, it was baseless promises without an end in sight.

And somehow, that seems to be the kind Kevin loves to give. Promises he never follows through with. Then, when I asked later, he'd sweep them under the rug, calling them *promises of yesteryears*, gone unnoticed, unredeemed. Then he would crack a lame-ass joke and change the topic.

Furiously, I scribbled my reminder-cum-request onto the sheet of paper that lay on the double quaver-shaped fur pillow. I held it up in the fluorescent lighting.

> *1. Remember the gift I got you at that gift shop? That was the first gift I ever gave to you. You promised to get me one from that gift shop* ***doh***. *Could you do that today?*

> *~ Megan*

There. I said it. Or rather, *I wrote it.*

It just still didn't look quite right to me. Maybe it was the harsh white light against the white paper that unsettled me, but I wasn't pleased with the results.

The words were acceptable; I said what I said, and there was no changing that, but I... it seemed like something was off.

"The pink index cards would have been perfect for this," my mind quipped, and I couldn't agree more.

There was a catch, though. The cards were in my former bedroom, and I wasn't very keen on going back there. How could I possibly handle that? Imagine Kevin now sees me creeping around and goes to tell his new girl that I'm crazy. His actions would be justified!

Deep down, I knew I did not give a rat's ass about whatever he was going to say about me or whatever Karen— or was it, Kelly– may think. The fact was that I was scared.

What exactly was I scared of? What was it that I couldn't face in particular?

This house was every inch still my abode, for the time being at least. My properties were still in that room I was too terrified to breach.

You may wonder what could lie behind that door that could be so terrifying. But the fact is, just looking into the face of the man who was once the center of your world and now has forcefully withdrawn could be one of the greatest terrors the human heart could ever experience. It could be likened to a nightmare, and in a flash, my life had become one. A cold, scary nightmare.

I was at the door of the room before I even realized it. Not giving in to cold feet, I turned the knob, and the door opened noiselessly.

My eyes roamed the warmly lit room for the silhouette of my stack of index cards, but they were no longer on the dresser where I had left them. *He had probably moved it to the bedside drawer then.*

Kevin slept peacefully on his chest, still having his work shirt on, seeing as I was no longer there to help him take it off and insist on his wearing his jammies. Maybe it's the freedom he craved. Perhaps I stifled him and cuddled him a bit too much.

I tore my eyes away from his six-foot-two frame and began to make my way to the bedside drawer. It was hard resisting the urge to sit on the bed, so I gave in, sat, and slid the first drawer open.

I felt the sensation of a familiar weight reaching out and encircling my waist. I nearly jumped out of my skin at the shock.

Kevin was indeed a creature of habit. He had stretched out his hand in his sleep to hold me like he used to when I wrote in bed, using the bedside drawer as a mini workstation.

His hand around me made me feel secure, but it did not feel quite right. I felt like I was stealing something that belonged to someone else. A touch that now belonged to another woman…

"Hey…Kelly…"

My ears could not have been playing such insane tricks on me. I swiveled to face him and found him deeply asleep.

Even in his dreams, it's her he calls for. Understood.

I snatched up the cards and removed his hand from my body. The hand that once strummed me more than his guitar had now become the hand of a stranger– one whose touches were foreign.

The lump in my throat made it rather difficult to swallow, and the stinging in my eyes had blurred the perimeters of my vision, forcing me to rely on memory as I found my way out of the room.

I leaned against the wall, deeply hurt by Kevin's sleep-talking. It shattered my heart all over again, just hearing how easily her name rolled off his tongue in such deep sleep.

My chest heaved with not just the intensity of the sobs but the pain deep-seated somewhere in my chest. It was probably the pain from having my heart broken by a man who was in a different reality zone altogether.

It hurt—a lot.

I let the tears roll down my cheeks on their own accord, defiantly making my way to the living room, where I rewrote the earlier message, now on the pink card.

It felt like I would go crazy cooped up in there. So I got changed for a morning run and then waited till 5:35 am before setting out.

I ran nearly five blocks with loud music blasting through my earphones, desperately trying to override the hurt with the sound of the music and the weariness of my heart. I exerted myself, forcing my muscles to keep charging ahead.

My running had very little to do with exercise or keeping fit. I ran like I could escape myself and my harsh reality. I ran like I could outpace the black hole that threatened to swallow me whole. For a chance to redeem the promises of yesteryears, I ran.

Unable to keep up at that pace, I skidded to a stop as I was out of breath already. The cold autumn morning breeze felt like tiny needles with each sharp air intake.

People had begun to mill about– other morning joggers or runners like myself and people who had to commute to work.

Never had I been so close to home yet felt so lost.

My exhausted limbs meandered into an alley and folded up on their own accord, forcing me just to sit there and hug my knees.

I rested my head on the peaks of my knees, letting the noise of the rousing city wash over me, intermingling with the now soft music in my ears, gently lulling me to sleep.

A gentle hand tapped my shoulder, rousing me from the uneasy sleep I had fallen into.

"Are you okay?"

Eyes nearly swollen shut from crying, I tried to see the face of who it was that was speaking to me so kindly. The sun was already overhead, so all I could make out was the silhouette of his face.

He helped me up before asking again in a soothing voice that made me almost start bawling about all my life's issues, "Are you okay?"

I nodded slowly, wondering how long I had slept.

"Were you jumped or something?"

The man had a characteristically aquiline nose and a gentleness about him that I found so reassuring. It was a battle trying to keep my guard up.

"Um, ah... no. Thanks for asking... I just uh...fell asleep. By the curb. Not unusual."

I let out a nervous chuckle. He smiled. A small, sincere smile that wasn't too broad to be disconcerting and not so small that it would strike me as fake. His very dark hair had an uncanny resemblance to mine– in its natural state.

"Certainly. Not unusual at all." We shared a look before he continued, "In case you ever want to talk to someone, you could ring me up. Here, if you don't mind," handing me a black business card he seemed to whip out of nowhere. *Hmm, mysterious. Seems interesting.*

Out of courtesy, I collected it. Not like his smooth talking and suaveness had any effect on me, I was just being courteous.

"Thank you."

"Do have a lovely day, Runner of the Alleyway."

I cocked my head at his retreating back, spluttering from trying to hold back my laughter. The universe sure went out of her way to brighten up my day. I could only wonder what else she had in store for me.

By the time I got home, of course, the apartment was empty as Kevin had gone to work. His dishes from the scrambled eggs and toast breakfast he had sat in the sink, and I had half the mind not to touch it.

I glanced at the center table. It was empty save for the vase of flowers. *Good. That means he got my note.*

By noon, I was so pumped that I had already completed two of the three articles I was to submit. I decided to cook dinner as soon as I was done with the third.

I was in a relatively good mood, so I tried to be as productive as possible before a reality check whacked me across the face.

Dinner was going to be penne pasta with vodka sauce and some parmesan cheese. Kevin loves his cheese. He'd say, "There's no such thing as too much cheese!" in that funny singsong voice.

My smile faltered a little when I realized that I might never get to hear him say that again.

I was working on the third article when I heard Kevin clear his throat in the living room. I was shocked. I did not hear the elevator bell ding, nor did I hear him enter the room.

His hair was slightly messy; maybe it was– *what was her name now? Ah, yes, Kelly–* Kelly's doing. I grit my teeth, forcing myself to look past that.

He looked like he had something to say, and he should since he got my note this morning. He merely stood there, watching me, an awkward staring contest going on between us. He probably wanted me to ask for it. The egotistical bastard.

"Where is it?"

The words were like lead in my mouth. There. I did what he wanted. I've spoken up and asked for it.

He looked at me coolly, his expression fluctuating between amusement, disdain, and feigned confusion. It stung.

"Where is what?"

"I believe you saw my note?"

He merely raised his eyebrows and shrugged. He set his grey bike against the wall before going on to say, "I didn't get it. No amount of gifts is going to change anything, Megan. The earlier you realize this, the better."

What the hell was this man raving about? What does he mean by no amount of gifts... was that what I was doing?

I didn't want to think about that then. My eyes were already starting to sting, so I quickly moved on to the next thing I had to say.

"Kevin, I made you dinner. Would you like to eat now, or would you want to freshen up first?"

A sly smile akin to a smirk crept along his face. But as quickly as it appeared, it disappeared.

"No. Don't bother. I ate already."

Oh, that's why. Indignation filled my very bones, and I felt myself get increasingly angry. How dare he not acknowledge my efforts and try to evade me at every turn? If not anything, was I not the woman he once loved? Was I not a person worthy of respect too?

He started walking away, and I followed him.

"What did I do to you that was so wrong, huh?" I swallowed the fast-forming lump that threatened to impair my speech. "I know I'm not perfect, but I gave you everything I know how to give. How could you be with someone for seven years and not even care enough about them to pick up a silly little trinket on the way home from work?"

He only looked at me blankly as though tuned out from the conversation.

Okay, that's enough.

I pushed my way into the room, our formerly shared room, and snatched the duvet and my favorite double quaver pillow before heading back to the guest room that had now become my prison.

I sobbed, the wound in my heart gaping and sore. Curled up into a ball on the floor, I wish I'd just shrink and disappear. The grief was already making me see and hear things.

I thought I heard footsteps at my door. I debated opening the door and looking out like a crazy lady, only to see nothing out there. I had acted desperate enough. No chance in hell would I let myself look like a fool any longer.

Not now. Not anymore.

Chapter 7

Kevin

♥

Day Two: Thursday

I was going to pass by. The gift shop was once again in front of me, beckoning, reminding me of Megan's request. I didn't want to get her a gift, not anymore. My mind was like a pendulum, swinging to and fro between two extremes. If I did, Kelly wouldn't be too pleased. She was of the opinion that Megan was trying to manipulate me. Was she really? Maybe she was. She was trying to make me feel nostalgic to the extent that I would be willing to work things out with her. Nostalgia. The word had been reoccurring in my head lately.

But what if she was not? What if she was genuinely looking for some sort of closure? Looking at me, wondering if I could help give that to her. But she had done nothing, if it was closure she wanted, why shouldn't I offer her that at least?

I stood in front of the shop now. As I backed them, the cars driving past me were honking, with the drivers shouting expletives at each other. But there was a still wind blowing, slightly hitting the side of my face and blowing against my shirt. I could see into the shop as the door was transparent, light falling on various items I couldn't quite decipher from the side I was on. Like being in a dream with the details blurry and out of reach.

The shop owner was seated on a stool to the right of the entrance. He was a bespectacled old man with his hair and mustache grey. He looked like something straight out of animation, some sort of wise, benevolent king with a beautiful daughter-slash-princess.

I summoned courage and went in. The shop owner raised his head from the book he was reading and focused his large eyes on me, making me feel like I was under scrutiny, a pathogen under the magnifying power of a light microscope. Then, he blinked, and the spell was broken.

"What can I do for you, sir?" he inquired.

I didn't know what to say. I hadn't made up my mind yet on what to get her.

"Looking for something for your wife?"

My head snapped in his direction as he said it. I was already scanning the shop for what l could give Megan. I saw antique books, some wristwatches, rare oddities that I couldn't identify, and even lightbulbs.

"Yes. Something like that." I lied. I couldn't exactly tell him that I cheated and my wife had caught me, and all this was an attempt at a peaceful breakup.

"You guys got married?"

I felt like my neck was going to snap with the way I kept looking back at him as he kept saying things that made me think there was another meaning to his words.

"Yes...She's my wife; that means we're married." I answered him hesitantly.

He laughed silently, his mustache vibrating in tune with his laughter. His eyes crinkled, his face's wrinkles showing how old he was.

"I get that reaction from people; I'm sorry. I remember when your lady came here some years ago. She got you a watch."

Then, he turned his face back to the book he was reading, leaving me entranced.

"You remembered the time we came here?"

He glanced at me, and his lips curled up. I was starting to think this was all a ruse, but it was too accurate to be that.

"Nobody comes here anymore. At least, not for the last decade. I tend to remember the ones that I do. But Megan came by once in a while to say hello. She doesn't come anymore, and I can see why. Is she happy? Such a nice girl."

His eye didn't leave me now. Boring into my face, staring into the depths of my soul, as if daring me to lie and say she was happy and in good spirits. To say that our marriage was a success and we were celebrating our anniversary, hoping for many more years of happiness and health.

"Erm... I was hoping to get her a gift for our anniversary."

"You don't know what to get her? What are you doing here, then? There are other places where you could get her something nicer than the trash you see here."

I blinked. He was brutally honest. I didn't know how to face that. I had been dodgy and anything but honest for almost a year, deceiving Megan when I could have come clean. I felt guilt and contrition. No one deserved that.

"The first time she got me a gift, it was from right here. So for our anniversary, I wanted to get her something from here too."

His smile had turned sad. He looked like he was reminiscing too. Indeed, he couldn't see that I was lying. She had almost begged me to get her something, and it was certainly not something I had thought of myself. I didn't even bother getting her anything.

"Ah! Young love. My wife was like that. She demanded gifts for everything. Valentine, mother's day, her birthday, our anniversary, and children's day."

I couldn't help laughing.

"You must be so happy."

"No. She died seven years after we got married. I've never looked at another woman since. I couldn't throw away some of the gifts I got her. So, I put them here for sale. Maybe young people can use that to find love for themselves."

His story struck me. I saw the pain in his eyes, and I knew the intense sorrow he went through at her passing.

"I'm sorry."

This was probably the only real thing I had said since I walked through the glass doors. He nodded in acknowledgment, his face still a mask filled with sorrow. His mustache shook again, only this time I knew it was laughter that caused their motion. Then, he removed the watch he was wearing, paused for a moment, and gave it to me.

His face had the smile back. I didn't understand.

"Why are you giving that to me?"

"Look at it."

I recognized it at once. It was like mine, a replica. I looked at him for an explanation.

"My father made watches, and he gave this pair to Helen and me when we got married. I decided to give the other to Megan, and it's only fitting that I give this one to you."

My hand closed over the watch gratefully. If there ever was a gift that I could get Megan, this was it.

"How much am I to pay for this?"

I was afraid that he wouldn't want me to pay for it. I wanted to give him something, at least. The watch held sentimental value for him. But he refused all payment attempts.

"Extend my greetings to Megan."

I turned away from him, not knowing what to make of that interaction with the shop owner. He never told me his name too. As I left, he called to me.

"Sort things out with her, Mister. Good afternoon."

Then, he turned back to his book. He knew.

On the train to work, I looked at the watch again. There was no one in the seat beside me, so I had a bit of privacy. It was truly identical to mine. I couldn't give her the watch like that, though. Megan wouldn't like it. She would want it to be wrapped with wrapping paper that had flowery designs. I still had some in my briefcase.

I decided to add a note to it too.

Thanks for all the good times we shared.

~Kevin

I felt good after I did all that. It was a little price to pay for whatever I did, for the way it broke her heart even though I was following mine. I put the watch in my briefcase and closed it. I was already late for work.

Kelly was waiting by the door to my office. There were lines of worry on her face. I understood. I had never been late in one year. The last time I was late was the first time we started getting closer. The day before, Megan had told me she was going to attend a writer's conference. I had come back from work and expected her to be back too. She had texted me, telling me she was home already.

So I got home and not seen her anywhere. I came in and called her name. There was no answer, no reply; the house was silent. I assumed she wasn't home and decided to call her. Her phone was right on the table. Then, I proceeded to recheck the house. Everywhere was empty. Her office was locked. She wasn't in, but she never went anywhere without her phone.

I scoured the block and asked our neighbors about her whereabouts. She was nowhere to be found. I started panicking. I called the police, but they said what they always said to those in my position. They couldn't commence a search for anyone unless they were missing for twenty-four hours or more. I didn't know what else to do. I didn't want to call her parents; alarming them was the last thing I wanted.

Then, when it was almost three in the morning, I heard the door to her office open. She was inside there the whole time, with her *Sony* headset over her head, writing. She had completely lost track of time and looked quite refreshed. She hadn't bothered to check if I was home or if dinner was made. She sat there, locked herself in, and went to work like nothing else mattered.

I was happy to see that she was safe, at least. But at the same time, I was enraged. She didn't notice my anger until the next day when the police came, and the neighbors inquired about the incident. It was then she realized the extent of what her negligence had caused. But that wasn't what made me angry; at least, that wasn't all of it.

She was so single-minded that she failed to realize that there were things that needed to be taken care of. That wasn't her first time. That was the straw that broke the camel's back. She didn't also seem to understand what I was angry about. In her words, she was working just like anybody else.

But Kelly understood when she saw me looking like what the cat dragged in the morning following the incident. She listened as I poured out my mind, and that was the beginning of her stealing my heart. She didn't, for once, fail to see when I was in trouble or disturbed. That was what I was missing in my marriage. Megan expected me to have control over anything, but I was only human. Very soon, I started confiding in Kelly, and it felt... perfect.

She looked worried again. I didn't want to lie to her, so it was better she didn't know about it.

"I'm sorry, babe."

I gave her a quick kiss on the cheek to try and appease her. It didn't work as well as I thought it would, but it was okay for the moment. She would come back to it later. I walked into my office, and she followed closely. I put my briefcase under my table, refraining from calling any attention to it. I was supposed to work on files I brought from home, but she was hovering over my shoulder.

"What are you hiding in your briefcase, Kevin?" she questioned, curt and acidic.

I should have known it was futile to hide anything from her. She knew me completely. I raised the briefcase to the table. I must have looked guilty. This was something Megan wouldn't have noticed. My palms were a bit sweaty, and I didn't want her to know that I went against her wishes and got Megan what she wanted.

"What is it, Kev?"

She had softened up. It was a ruse to get me to talk about what was bothering me. I knew, and she knew that I knew. Our eyes met, and understanding passed across her eyes to mine, her eyes always twinkling with laughter, eyes that loved looking at me. She knew, or she had guessed.

I put my sweaty hands and brought the watch, wrapped up like a valentine's gift. She took it from me and gave it back without a second glance. She was hurt, and I knew it.

"You said you weren't going to get her anything." She accused me.

I was at a loss for words. How could I explain to her the turmoil and guilt I felt after I faced her? She would try to, but she wouldn't understand.

"It was the least I could do."

The failure of words to fully convey my thoughts and emotions. I reached for her, supplicating, willing her to understand. She was hurt that I would return to what I promised her. But she got over it quickly. She steeled herself, stood upright, and broadened her shoulders. She looked proud and majestic.

"Don't agree to anything she says again. You hear me, Kev?"

She was half-pleading and half-commanding now. I nodded. I couldn't say yes after I went back on my promise yesterday. So I nodded. She slammed the door on her way out.

When I got home, Megan had retired for the night. I had visited the gym before coming over, and Kelly had insisted I put the condoms in my pocket again. She wanted to send a message to Megan. But there was no need, not tonight. She was sleeping peacefully; I watched the rise and fall of her bosom for a while before I went to my bedroom, the smile on her face as she slept engraved in my memories.

I walked over to the kitchen and put it on the counter. She came here every morning and was bound to see it. I didn't give it much thought and went back to sleep.

Chapter 8

Megan

♥

Day Two: Thursday

L ife is funny in that it does not come with alerts telling you to enjoy the time you are currently spending with someone. Life would not tell you that these experiences would go on to become core memories intertwined with our existence and very sense of self.

Life is a delicate, not-so-funny paradox.

I lay there on the ground holding on to the duvet for dear life, angry with myself because somehow, I still craved the scent of this man that had hurt me so much.

I was angry and pained; beyond the hurt, I felt stupid. Stupid not to have seen the signs. Stupid for sacrificing so much only to get the short end of the stick. Stupid, still, for very nearly deferring to him, even with his cheating and all.

It isn't his fault at all; no, it isn't. It is all mine. I was probably too agreeable, too subservient, too... pliable. Was that it? Is that the reason he won't look at me anymore, without disgust tainting what used to be pure adoration?

I dragged myself up from the cold floor and stumbled into bed.

The carton was still where I had dragged it out from, with its contents mostly scattered. A hammer, a drill, and the remaining sheets of paper from this morning's writing dilemma, among other things, lay next to the box.

Me, with a disorderly room? It's almost unthinkable. Am I already becoming that which I hate? I think not.

I crouched to pick up the tools and bits that lay strewn about the room. Balls of scrunched-up paper were also in the mix, and I felt a tiny tinge of shame for being such a slob.

I was going to put the hammer and drill back in when I felt my hand graze a thick envelope. I pulled on it, causing the edge to rip a bit. Some of the envelope's contents fell out, and I could not help but wonder at the timing.

They were pictures of Kevin, some of his friends, and me on one of his birthdays. I could not quite remember the exact year, but I remember word for word, the promises he made all those many years ago.

I shuffled through the pictures. There was one of him being fist-bumped by Jake and Tony, twin friends of his who moved to the East Coast later that year.

Striped t-shirts were all the rage then, preferably layered over and under other tops. I laughed at what I was wearing in the pictures; a striped crop top and low rise boot cut denim. It was now so out of touch with the modern trends.

That couldn't have bothered me, though. What wouldn't I give to have him look at me with the same intensity as he looked at me in that photo booth so many years ago?

In another picture, our foreheads touched– the classic lovebirds pose. He wouldn't have ever dreamed that there would come a day when he'd admit to falling out of love with me, but life happens.

One of the pictures captured him lifting me with a large, infectious grin plastered on his face. He was pointedly ensuring my weight wasn't on the black strap watch he had on his right wrist, and rightfully so.

I spent a lot of time in that gift shop on Main and 15th, trying to select the kind of timepiece I believed my man deserved. It was a handmade watch from the House of Horology, a pricey one at that. I knew how long I had to save up to get Kevin that watch. I remember taking extra shifts just to ensure that ten thousand dollars were complete.

I had looked at many watches, but only this one, a unique handmade watch from the House of Horology, caught my eye. I didn't know the price at the time, but I just wanted to get him that exact watch. I even paid extra to have his full name engraved on it.

He said he'd cherish it and ensure that nothing untoward ever happened to it, and on that, he has kept his word. He made me tell him where I bought his gift and then promised to get me something also from that gift shop.

I smiled, the pictures evoking bittersweet memories that I didn't even realize I had.

I recall standing in front of the shop, all shy and very unsure of myself. I didn't think someone like myself would ordinarily have business with such a high-end gift store like that. Except that I was seeing a high-end man– that's what Kevin had always been to me– and I wanted to get him something befitting on his birthday, at least.

I lurked outside for nearly a century and a half until an observant staff spotted me. An older, bespectacled man waved at me from inside the shop.

"Hello, I couldn't help but notice you standing there. Would you like to make a purchase?"

Usually, it would not have been very comfortable, but the way this lady said it, I would have almost thought she was inviting me for freebies. It wasn't in the least bit offensive or awkward. I remember wishing to have her kind of effortless confidence.

"...Or are you waiting for someone?"

"Umm, no... I want to make a purchase, actually. I was just trying to work up the confidence to walk inside."

Her smiles put me at ease and kept the nervousness at bay for a moment there. "It really does be like that sometimes."

"So, who are you getting something for? Is it for a birthday, wedding anniversary, baby shower..."

The interior of the store was practical yet classy, with some things arranged on racks, yet some others kept behind tempered glass. They sold a wide range of gifts, from diamond jewelry to Chelsea boots, to china and confetti.

Everything Gifts was an apt name for that store indeed. I glanced around; the sheer luxury that surrounded me suddenly made me feel very small. What was I thinking, coming to such a great place as this? I was going to embarrass myself for sure. I steered clear of the aisles. What if I break something?

"...so have you decided on what you'd be getting?"

The lady's chirpy voice jolted me back to the present, forcing me to move my mouth and speak.

"Yes. A watch. For my man."

The lady gave a knowing smile. "Follow me, please."

She proceeded to show me a vast array of different makes of watches. They were so many, at first, I was overwhelmed. She took her time with me, explaining the pros and cons of each one. Not like I understood anything anyway, but I nodded, knowing that once I saw the one I felt suited his personality more, I'd know.

Well, my hunch was spot on. I saw the handmade watch with unique craftsmanship from the House of Horology, and I knew I just had to get it for him. There was a catch, though—the price. I did the math immediately. I'd have to do double shifts at the two places I worked and throw in my savings. The joy on his face when I came back a month later with him by my side to pick up the gift made my sacrifice feel totally worth it. If it's for Kevin, it was worth it. But now, was it really?

I put the pictures away and clambered into bed, once again wishing to disappear into the wafts of the fabric.

I soon found myself walking down the street alone, with no single being in sight. The wind howled, blowing debris, leaves, and unanchored objects about. I don't know where I was headed, but it had to have been very important to make me set out in that boisterous weather. Was it just a windy day, or that is a storm gathering momentum by the minute?

The clouds were dark, and lightning flashed in the distance. It seemed like I was strolling through a ghost town. As if it were not enough, I could hear growling but couldn't pinpoint the location it was emerging from.

I ran as fast as I could desperately from the storm and the beasts in the tornado and back to my house; wherever

I was going to needed to wait. My survival was of utmost importance.

I exerted myself so much trying to evade the storm, yet I felt very slowed down, and the heavy winds were starting to gain on me already.

Just two more houses before my apartment building... I should be able to–

I never got to finish that thought as I got flung against the asphalt, stunning me. The ground was suddenly all up in my face, and my head gave a low thrum. The next thing I felt was a sharp pain. I looked back only to see dark, wispy claws like smoke digging into my leg, the pain excruciating enough to jolt me awake from that terrible nightmare.

I sat up straight in bed, panting, my heart beating wildly against my rib cage. My mouth felt dry, and my head hurt a lot. That dream felt somewhat too real for a nightmare of that magnitude. I needed a glass of water, but even I was scared to put weight on that leg.

Gingerly, I put one foot down. No pain. Great. I shuffled to the kitchen to find some aspirin tablets and, more importantly, water. I downed both and sat on the kitchen floor, leaning on the cabinets.

A glance at the wall clock told me it was nearly eleven. Kevin would have been back from work and gone to sleep in what used to be our bedroom. He couldn't expect me to stay with him there anyway, and I could care less about whether or not he came home tonight. But I was thirsty. I would have a drink and maybe check him, if I could.

The kitchen was neat. He hadn't touched anything. *Great.* I rummaged in the fridge for something that could help me sleep better. I settled on orange juice.

I set the box of orange juice on the counter and went to fetch a glass. I was filling my glass when I raised my eyes and found myself staring at a small, floral-print gift bag.

I was shocked and stopped pouring the juice. I blinked a couple of times to be sure I wasn't hallucinating or still dreaming. The lavender bag still sat pretty on the counter, watching me internally assure myself that I didn't see things.

A small gift bag. *He got it for me.*

I opened it and brought out the nude vegan leather case. At first, I thought he was returning his since I was the one who got it for him. So I peeked at the metal disc beneath to check for his name– Kevin Stewart– but it was blank. It was only then I noticed this one had thinner straps.

His was different and the same–it was a replica, but with thinner straps– the feminine version. Maybe Mr. Rogers had this set lying around in his shop. But I didn't expect Kevin to get me the watch; it was a pleasant surprise.

Then I saw the little note in the bag.

Thanks for all the good times we shared.

~Kevin

I couldn't help it. The tears started flowing on their own, running across my face and dropping onto the counter.

It wasn't a long note, but it was profound, all the same. *Was this what I really wanted? Was this what I really craved?*

I thought of a response to him for a bit while I searched for my favorite black gel pen.

I couldn't find it, so I took a pen I found in the drawer and one of the index cards and wrote on it, dropping it for him on the center table as usual.

As I went, I shuffled back to my room in a slight daze, and I clutched the watch, still inside its nude leather box in the floral-print cellophane bag, unable to believe my luck.

I wondered if his next assignment would make him learn something new or at least remind him of yet another promise he was yet to fulfill.

The words I wrote on that card played in my mind as I made my way to my room;

> *2. Remember, years ago, you told me you wanted to be a successful musician singing worldwide, and I always dreamed about you being a singer performing in front of a crowd.*

*You always assured me that it was something
you'd eventually do but still...*

*If you could choose what will become of me,
what would you have wanted me to be? Do gift
me something **Rel**ated to that.*

~ Megan

My words were direct, I know, but knowing Kevin, his
ego is also probably hurting from me not communicating
my appreciation for the watch. And that, I won't.

Chapter 9

Kevin

♥

Day Three: Friday

There were a variety of cameras to choose from. There were so many types at the store, with different prices and models too. But those weren't the things on my mind at that moment.

I was thinking about when Megan got me that guitar. I couldn't believe my eyes. It was the most excellent surprise anyone had brought me in a while.

"I can't take this."

I told her. She had laughed it off. I knew how much guitars like that cost. I wondered how much work she had to do, the extra shifts, and I didn't know what else to say.

"I'll pay you back. I promise."

She frowned then. She had always warned me against planning to repay her.

"I didn't get it so that you could repay me. I love you, Kev. I. Love. You. I'll do more if I can."

She told me not to worry about it and that she just liked making people smile.

"Well, you're good at it," I told her.

Then her eyes had gone dreamy as she said, "If only I could capture all the smiles and put them in my pocket. Now that would be something."

That was why I was here. This wasn't exactly "putting them in her pocket," but photography was something I thought Megan might be good at. She had a way of bringing out the joy and natural beauty in everyone. With a fancy camera in hand, she'd be able to collect every smile she came across in stunning high definition.

Remembering what she did once again, there was no way I wouldn't have won that competition. With the guitar in my hands, I saw her in the crowd cheering me on. The feeling of the crowd listening to me and singing along was like nothing I had ever experienced.

I had always wanted to sing, everyone thought I had a good voice, but my father would have none of it. He warned that it wasn't something you could hold and give to your children. He believed in studying at college, getting out with a degree, and going to work regular hours like other people. I had believed him, although I still liked testing out at competitions like the one I won.

But I had to go see Kelly at the gym. She had been sending me lots of messages as I didn't show up on time. Maybe I would change my mind before I came back. But even as I thought that, I realized that I didn't want to. I walked out of the store, ignoring the cold stare of the store attendant. I had other things to settle first.

I met Kelly in front of the gym, and it seemed she was always waiting for me these days. This time, my face wasn't guilty. I had not done anything. Kelly was wearing a black tracksuit with her hair packed into a bun. She looked beautiful as always. Her lithe frame was accentuated by the drape of the tracksuit she was wearing. Hers was a face that could easily be called cute, her big brown eyes very similar to a curious child's.

It was hard thinking about anyone being cruel to her, but that was what her ex did. They had been dating for seven years straight out of college, like Megan and me.

He was a doctor, which meant he had a very tight schedule but Kelly being as nice as she was– always had dinner prepared for him any time he was through with his shifts. She had thought everything was going well and was waiting for him to propose, but he never did. Until one day, he stopped coming home.

When it happened the first night, she had thought he was held up at work, even when he didn't pick up her calls. When he didn't return the second night, she had called the hospital to check if he was around. That was when the storm broke. There was nobody named Dr. Thompson working with them. She didn't understand, even when there were withdrawals from their credit cards to the tune of thousands of dollars. She had erroneously thought she was the victim of another credit card fraudster that somehow got her details.

Until she went to the police to report it, it was there that she knew the range of her boyfriend's plan. Kelly didn't need to work, and her parents were millionaire oil moguls that catered to her every need and placed her on a CEO's salary. But she opened a joint account with Thompson, who waited for the right time before going away with most of the money in the account.

But Kelly didn't care much for money. Her heart was broken, and she couldn't face her parents. They had warned her against moving in with him, but she had refused advice. They hadn't approved of him, and she had moved in anyway. Her mum was livid, but it was her dad that helped her out of the financial dilemma that Thompson put her in. It was years ago, but she told me she hadn't had any relationship with anyone since the incident.

Now, it didn't matter. I didn't care about her money, and I only cared that we loved each other and were willing to do anything to be together. That was why I didn't think it was a good idea to tell her that Megan had made another request.

"She asked for something else."

Kelly was backing me as we walked into the gym. The part of the gym that was reserved for VIPs. It was almost always secluded, and during times like that, we had privacy. There was a swimming pool and an exclusive room for the VIPs. Kelly had got me a premium membership slot.

I could feel her roll her eyes in disgust. She continued walking as she talked to me over her back, the echoes of her feet as she walked, putting some feeling of dread into my bones. Before long, I felt the familiar shiver of apprehension that she would know that what I wanted to do was what she wouldn't want me to.

"No way. No damn way. What did you say, Kev?"

She was walking faster now, the echoes becoming more strident and increasing in pitch like her anger.

"I haven't gotten anything, Kelly. Calm down."

Well, I wasn't exactly lying, but I wasn't telling the truth either. She looked appeased as a smile formed on her face.

"What did you tell her?" She inquired.

"I couldn't tell her anything. She dropped a note. Should I reply on the note too?"

She nodded, fully satisfied now.

"Come swim with me."

I was back at the store. The attendant must have been thinking I was some sort of customer who couldn't decide if he wanted to buy or not, spending his whole time trying to decide and then failing to get anything.

But as I left the gym, I headed straight for the store. I had promised to pay Megan back for the guitar she got me. I still had the guitar in my cupboard at the apartment with some strings missing. I was going to pick up singing again. I was going to fix the guitar strings and tune them. I would love to see how much vocal agility I have left. I sure must have gone rusty somewhat.

There was no denying it– I sure was excited.

I had lied to Kelly, but that was a small price to pay for repaying Megan. Besides, she didn't need to know. I knew her, and she would have done the same thing in my shoes. But here I was, standing before the cameras, and one thing I hadn't noticed before was the price tags. They were high. At least higher than I could remember.

Then again, I remembered how Megan must have gotten the guitar without any prompting from me, working extra shifts to get something she knew I wanted but couldn't get. I took one of the most expensive cameras they had on display, a Canon 5D DSLR, and went to the attendant. He looked impressed. I got out of there before I could change my mind. I was starting to think the camera I got was more expensive than I wanted.

Megan knew quite a lot about cameras, and getting her one this expensive might give her hope that I wanted to amend things that were far from what I wanted. I didn't want to have to dash her hopes when I went back to Kelly. I would apologize to her later on for the lie I told. I also knew that that wouldn't be the last time I would continue lying to her if I allowed Megan to keep asking for requests. Not like they were really requests, though. They were more like reminders of things I had once promised yet hadn't followed up on, so yeah, I feel a bit guilty.

I think she was using my guilt against me, and she was using it well. I remembered Sloane, the girl I was dating before I met Megan. I rarely talked about her. She was a master at guilt-tripping and twisting my emotions to suit her whims and devices. I went along for a while until I couldn't take it anymore.

We had a class at college, and she didn't show up. I was worried and went to see her. I met her in his arms, kissing and making out right on the couch I got her. He was my friend. But that wasn't the end. She followed me to my apartment, begging, claiming she loved me.

Looking back now, I see how foolish I was. She threatened to kill herself if I left her. I took that as evidence that she was sorry and we didn't break up. She knew I could easily forgive and used that to her advantage. The next time I caught her was at a party we were invited to by one of our friends with another guy. There was no excuse, but I was heartbroken. I was weak and couldn't make hard decisions. But not anymore.

Maybe I am a hypocrite using the things my ex did as a yardstick to measure Megan and when I cheated too. But then again, it didn't matter. I wasn't going to grant any more requests.

I met her drinking wine, with the bottle on the couch and a sitcom playing on the television. The expression on her face was a far cry from the comedic mood of the show she was watching. It was apparent her mind had strayed far. Far beyond the walls of this house even. Even I wasn't that clueless, and it didn't require extensive pondering to figure out what was on her mind.

I dropped the package on the table in front of her. She looked at me quizzically. She didn't understand what I was up to. As she opened it, I smiled. She looked like a three-year-old who was told that Santa came in the night bearing gifts. She couldn't hide her curiosity, and when she saw what I had bought, the smile that lit up her face made me glad, reminding me of who it once was...

We had our first official date on the beach. It was at night, and we were almost alone. There was another couple far to our left, but they left almost as soon as we came. I was nervous. I didn't want our first date to be clichés like those that went to the movies or a restaurant. I wanted something fun, so I chose the beach at night. The moon was out, so I thought we would watch the tide and eat the pasta we ordered.

It was a disaster. I should have looked at the weather forecast before choosing to go to the beach or even going out at all. The rain started suddenly and caught us unawares. The food was soiled with the rain mixed with sand from the beach. I had thought Megan would be looking for shelter. Not that there would be any, as the beach was virtually empty, but she started jumping around and laughing. She looked like a three-year-old then too. Without a care in the world, not caring about divorces or a cheating husband.

When she opened the package and saw that it was a camera, the goofy smile that appeared on her face was genuine and devoid of worry. Inside the pack was a brand new Canon 5D DSLR camera with a note.

For capturing smiles.

~ Kevin

She ran her fingers over it lightly and looked up at me. I could see the love in her eyes and wished I could reciprocate. But I couldn't stop myself from grinning from ear to ear. She looked so happy. I grabbed my phone and took a picture of her face like that, something to remind myself of the good times we shared, no matter the outcome of the divorce proceedings. She caught me doing that, and she asked, still smiling.

"Why did you do that?"

I had no honest answer I could give her. I shrugged. The grin was still on my face, refusing to wipe off.

"Come on. Your turn."

She didn't understand what I said at first, her right eyebrow lifting in a silent question. I pointed to the camera.

"Come on. Take a picture."

She hurried to her feet with the camera, eager to test it out. She fumbled with the settings for a while before finally getting the hang of it. She took a picture of me smiling, and I looked just as happy as she was. She saw it too and tried to kiss me. I wasn't shocked, but that destroyed the mood immediately.

She set the camera with muted thanks, looking forlorn again. She picked up the glass of wine she had been drinking and went into the spare bedroom. I sat on the couch and continued watching the sitcom she had abandoned; later on, she joined me on the sofa too.

It wasn't awkward anymore, and it was the silence of old companions.

Chapter 10

Megan

♥

Day Three: Friday

S ometimes you just look back at your past decisions and wonder if you were in total control of your senses when you took them. Most decisions look perfectly sensible until they are viewed in hindsight. I was starting to agree with this school of thought concerning my part-time job as a guidance counselor and Leyton High.

Yes, I write for a magazine in New York, and I also work on their editorial board, but I felt that should not stop me from maximizing my potential. You see, I have quite an interest in guiding people toward making the right decisions now and even in the long run. So five years ago, I first took a guidance and counseling course as a joke when Kevin suggested I'd be good at advising people. A year later, I got this job as a part-time guidance counselor at

Leyton High School, not far from here. It is practically two blocks away.

The end of the school year is fast approaching, and with that comes a whole lot of letter writing, meetings, giving advice, and a mountain load of correspondence to deal with. Needless to say, these past few days have been hellish. It has been a hassle trying to stay sane and on top of all my responsibilities.

I clearly was not on top of my marriage. I couldn't let the laxness that put the 'for worse' on my wedding vows to hamper the lives of these young people who have to come to me for guidance. Neither could I allow any one of my coworkers to see the pain shining through. Worse still, my students. Those had a knack for identifying who and who were struggling, and these kids were already experts in peddling stories.

As a guidance counselor, I get approached with myriad questions, sometimes on issues, I have experienced myself. I am usually careful, so I don't overshare, though, because they came to one for solutions, so one should not end up just churning out one sob story after the other. They came because they were confused about their sexuality and social life and had questions concerning their academics. And, by academics, I do not mean I was being badgered with invitations to tutor them in calculus, no. The bone of contention was getting into college, more specifically, what schools to apply to, what schools to accept and what schools would be best for the fields of their choice.

My desk was a haven of several college and university brochures, my work folder full of all sorts of reference letters, all neatly stacked and filed away. Extra inside scoop from some top schools from students who were Leyton Alumni themselves. I suspect some of the kids that come around only do it because they thoroughly enjoy the scoop. I never turn them away, though.

The fall season is usually the busiest time of the year for me since I took on this part-time job at Leyton. I had not found myself liking it much; if anything, I dreaded falling for this particular reason. But if my current soon-to-be-divorced state was anything to go by, the student needs at Leyton High served as an excellent distraction from the utter chaos that was fast becoming my life.

It was nice, for the first time since our anniversary, not to find my head wholly consumed by thoughts of Kevin, our marriage, what I did wrong, what I could have done better, if I was worth staying for, and all that bullshit nobody cares about. Instead, I was engrossed in drafting the reference letters for those little devils, advising the confused art major not to settle for a community college just because her girlfriend was going there– trust me, that was always a bad idea. *Always.*

Year in, and year out, I'd see teenage couples whose first choice of college would be the ones their significant others were applying to, without regard for their future goals and ambitions. There was a handful too, who chose not to go to college so they would never have to leave their high school sweethearts. Sweet, but not very wise. In the event that they split up, then what happens to the one who sacrificed everything? That bore a bit of a resemblance to my life story, and I would not wish my mistakes on any young person, so I try to advise them the best I can without seeming too pushy. It is their life, after all.

And this was mine. A deplorable, stinking mess.

If those teens struggling to make sense of their lives ended up being like me...then their struggle would be all for nothing.

I gripped the wine glass stem more firmly in my hand as though it was responsible for my predicament. A romantic sitcom was on, but apart from the occasional laugh tracks, I could not make out anything else. I was in that chair, in that house, but I was miles and miles away from that screen. Just like how Kevin was in my bed, in this house, but his heart was long gone for who knows how long.

I could relate a bit too much to the students who felt uncertain about their futures and had no idea where to go or what the future holds for them. All I can do, or instead, all I do, is give them the stats for admissions and acceptances, the opportunities their SAT scores can afford them, and then tell them to follow their hearts. At the end of the day, all that matters is what the heart chooses. The rest of the body will have to go along with the consequences– good or bad. If I was going, to be honest, it is most likely going to be bad.

I believe I had always gone with what my heart chose per time, but maybe that wasn't true. Perhaps I was so head over heels in love with Kevin– at such an early age, too– that I managed to convince myself that his wants were my wants. That his dreams were my dreams...and his desires, my desires. Maybe they were, perhaps they weren't.

The door slammed shut, jolting me from my deep thoughts. I jumped on my seat, nearly spilling wine on myself. I inspected the beige satin camisole I wore for any drops of wine. Satisfied that there was none, I looked up to see Kevin placing something on the table, exhaustion coloring his movements.

I was puzzled, seeing that it was only a tiny box wrapped in a brown paper he had dropped. I looked up at him for an explanation of some sort, but he said nothing and merely moved away from the table, leaving me with my confusion.

"It's yours. Open it," he said with amusement playing in his eyes.

I do remember asking him to get me something that represented what he would want me to be. I dragged the tip of my stiletto nail across the thin brown paper wrapping. It felt like a carton box within, so I ripped through the paper quickly, in haste to see what lay within all that wrapping.

A Canon 5D camera with an extra 50mm f/1.2 USM lens. Is this a dream?

I looked at Kevin, who looked nearly as excited as I was. *No way.*

"Tell me you didn't...."

He nodded, laughing a little. "Hmm...I did."

A small white note peeked out from the ripped brown paper.

For capturing smiles.

~ Kevin

It was a short note, but it spoke to me volumes. The room suddenly grew blurry as tears filled my eyes. I remember the first time I took a picture of him. He was impressed the picture came out pretty decent. I recall him saying something along the lines of, "You capture smiles, lady, but it seems to me that you've captured my heart." I doubt he remembers, though.

I have always had a keen interest in photography, borrowing friends' cameras then. I was saving up for mine, but things always came up that made me postpone it.

I was always entering photo contests even though I didn't win any, and it was just exciting for me to participate in them. It ended up being one of my neglected hobbies, even though I was pretty good at it.

Seeing this thoughtful camera gift from Kevin rekindled that spark...

A bright light suddenly flashed in front of me. Kevin took a picture of me. I could bet it would not come out right. I had the silliest smile on, and I quickly set my camera down to look at the photo of me he had taken on his phone.

"Why did you do that?" I asked him amidst giggles. He only shrugged, a lazy smile tugging at the corners of his heart-shaped mouth. It made him look incredibly cute. His smile was probably mirrored on my face as I could already feel my cheeks start to burn. He seemed to thoroughly enjoy watching me, seeing that he hadn't looked elsewhere since.

"Come on. Your turn," I heard him say. *My turn, how? What does he want from me? Does he want a selfie? Or am I supposed to get him a gift too? I don't know what I could get him... would he like a silk tie with a matching pocket square and cufflinks?*

I cocked my head, trying to determine what he truly meant by *my turn*. Was I expected to do something of some sort? *It had better not be something weird or embarrassing.*

He should not expect me to jump through hoops just because he got me a camera.

He pointed towards the table. My eyes followed his hand till it settled on the object grazing my fingertips. *Oh, the camera.*

"Come on. Take a picture."

Now, that made sense.

"Let me just...." I told no one, in particular, trying to adjust the settings to my preference. I was going to take a close-up picture of his face and one full-body photograph with the background blurred.

"Well, don't just stand there. Say cheese!"

He looked surprised to hear me say that, and that look of amusement was too genuine to pass up. I heard the shutter click and grinned, pleased with myself for catching that on camera. The lighting was slightly off, as I forgot to turn the flash on.

"Come on... For the little birdies! A nice, warm smile!"

Kevin threw back his head in laughter, giving me many expressions to take snapshots of.

It reminded me of the first time I coined the term. Kevin originally was not one to sit still or pose for pictures, but Jake had a Polaroid camera I had borrowed for a bit, and I intended to squeeze out all the images of him I could get within that time frame. He was not cooperating at first, fretting about what poses to do until I started hyping him up. Getting the poses nailed was one thing; getting him to smile properly– and no, I don't mean that awkward teeth-showing he tried to call a smile– was a hassle because I was looking for real smiles. He smiled properly when he was looking at me directly, but the minute I put a camera to his face, he would get all self-conscious, and the smile would look like something plucked out of an eighteenth-century cookbook.

These pictures came out nicely, though. The lighting was just fine, and most of his smiles were genuine this time. His eyes seemed to sparkle with delight, and the laugh lines on his face were a bit more noticeable. He could easily pass for a model with that great jawline.

Kevin had aged nicely, and I couldn't wait to see how he'd look when he got old, like, say, eighty.

I was all too aware of his presence as he was standing very close to me, our sides touching as I showed him the pictures of him I had just taken. His familiar sandalwood and pine scent filled my nostrils as if reminding me of the male in the room. I flipped too fast from a picture he was still looking at, so he held my finger and went back two images.

It felt like a live wire touched my fingers, and I could feel the sizzle of electricity run from my fingertips all the way to my spine. I shuddered, shocked my body could still respond so much to his touch.

There was a gaping warmth that needed to be filled, and the brush of his arm against the bare skin of my arm did not help matters at all.

Unable to restrain myself any further, I tilted my head to study his face. *The arch of his full brows. His honeyed hazel eyes seemed to beckon to me. That proud nose bridge I had run my fingers over a million times. His square jaw. Those shapely, luscious lips were slightly moist from the last time he had wet them.*

My fingers found their way into the nape of his hair and pulled his head close. He moved towards me naturally, leaning in.

Right before our lips touched, he froze.

"I can't."

I nodded, retracting my fingers from his neck like it had suddenly been set on fire.

"Yes, we shouldn't."

So badly. So badly, I wanted to kiss him, but there were walls now. Restrictions. The sudden realization that I was no longer allowed to do that hit me. It felt strange, weird...unreal.

Then it occurred to me that I hadn't said thank you yet for the camera. I raised the camera awkwardly, bidding the disappointment and embarrassment to disappear from my face.

"Thank you so much, Kevin. It means a lot to me."

He didn't say anything. He merely smiled and nodded. It was a friendly smile devoid of condescension or pity. At least, I was grateful for that. He did not try to treat me like some unfortunate woman who could not rein in her emotions.

The sitcom was still on, so we both sat down and watched it for a while in silence. By the end of the show, he had dozed off, fully donned in work clothes with part of his weight on my slim frame.

I was barely awake myself, so I let him lie down and lay next to him on the couch, letting him be the big spoon while he draped his hand over me.

Finding comfort even on that long sofa, we slept, just like in old times.

Sometime around four in the morning, I woke up and met Kevin's hand draped around me on the couch we fell asleep on. If I stayed there till daybreak, it sure was going to be awkward, and I could even get accused of trying to seduce him or something, so gingerly, I edged out of the couch, which was a bit hard because he was the big spoon.

I did not want to wake him up, but I would prefer that than be called unsavory names tomorrow. Or later in the day since it was a new day already. He didn't wake up anyway. He was out like a light and probably had a very stressful day.

Once upon a time, he would tell me of every single thing that made up the day until, slowly, those conversations dwindled and eventually trickled to a stop. I miss him being vulnerable to me, but I guess that phase is long past now. *Now I'm the past.*

I sighed, dragging myself to the spare bedroom that now served as my room and perched on its edge. If I was indeed his past, I should get all I was promised in the past, and he could be on his merry way and enjoy his new future.

No, I was not interested in splitting his life earnings or his money or anything. I just wanted him to be happy. He is happy with his newfound love but fulfilling his promises regardless.

He made those promises all those years ago. The least he could do was stand by them.

And about promises, one vividly stood out in my memory...

Chapter 11

Kevin

♥

Day Six: Monday

S he had another note on the table waiting for me. This was no more a concern for me. I realized that I wasn't afraid of what Kelly would think. She didn't have to know. There was a saying- What you know can't hurt you. It dropped in my head sometime during the night. Although this was stupid, as many things unknown have destroyed many, in a way, I felt the speaker was talking about ignorance of danger being beautiful on some level.

Maybe I was overthinking again. Ignorance was never bliss, but that didn't mean knowledge was either. I remembered the day she saw the condoms in my pocket. That was when everything changed, the day I lost control over everything, and they spiraled into madness. Maybe if she didn't know about my affair, I would perhaps have found a way to resolve everything peacefully. But that was wishful thinking at this juncture.

> *3. Remember our second anniversary when you took **Mi** out to dinner and said it would be a tradition in every one of our anniversaries? Four years have passed without you fulfilling that promise.*

> *So tonight, I'm reminding you...pick up dinner from our favorite restaurant.*

> *~ Megan*

Bingo's. I laughed out loud at the memory. I picked up my suitcase and went out. Bingo's was a Thai restaurant we went to when we were still dating, and we continued going there even after we were married. We only stopped about three weeks before Megan's discovery when we suddenly became too busy for date night. I remember the first night we braved Bingo's. The restaurant was relatively new, but we knew nothing about Thai food.

It was previously owned by someone we called Ben from Thailand. His original name was much harder to pronounce. After the first visit, we knew, or rather, we thought, we would never come back. I had only had nights free on weekdays, so we went on another date. This time, we decided to go somewhere we hadn't gone before.

It was a disaster. The food was great. It was hard to imagine anything better. My mother was an excellent cook, but it was hard to compare anything to Ben's cooking. Ben had a teenage boy that worked with him. For some reason, that day, the boy made a mistake and filled the dessert with pepper. Lots and lots of pepper. After the appetizer and main course were so good, we didn't expect anything less from the dessert. We left with our tongues burning and our eyes streaming.

But the food was so good that we decided to give Bingo's a second chance and revisit them. We were not disappointed. Then as I walked into the train, it occurred to me. Was Megan asking for a second chance just like we gave Bingo's? Or was this just a coincidence? She was going through our *greatest hits* and trying to make me remember how good we were.

It didn't matter right now. The fact was, I remembered already. We were good together. We were—*past tense.* There was no use trying to resurrect the dead. The last notes of the melody have since been strung out, and now there was no music left to dance to. It is life. It happens.

I decided to visit Bingo's on my way back from work. I wanted to enjoy the serenity and be alone, thinking about the good times Megan and I shared at this spot. I didn't know that would be possible as there was one problem. Kelly decided to tag along. Somehow, I had let slip that I wasn't going straight home and needed to go somewhere to unwind.

"Then, I'm coming with."

And that was that. I didn't have a say in the matter. Somehow, I managed to fake a smile to mirror hers while thinking about how to avoid her company. I should have known Kelly. She wasn't backing down. I closed late, and she waited for me in my office. Now we were at the restaurant. She was all smiles and holding my hand. It was almost as if she wanted to stake her claim on me.

There were a lot of things I didn't tell her these days, many developments she had no idea about. She didn't know that Bingo's, which was once a little shack on an unknown street, was now a remarkable chain of restaurants nationwide, and the one Megan and I frequented, the one we were headed to now, was the headquarters. We used to eat there frequently, so they knew us pretty well.

When we entered, we were immediately moved to a table. Kelly was ecstatic.

"Their customer service is very good, Kev. How did you know about this place? You used to come here before?"

She kept on talking, but I wasn't listening. I was starting to notice the stares of the servers on duty. Megan was close with all of them. Every time Ben was around, he made sure he spoke with us whenever we were around too. So, for the servers to see me with another woman looking cozy, it was bound to raise a few questions and was definitely a topic for gossip.

Kelly was being her usual lively self, chattering on and on about how we loved Thai food and had no idea there was such a lovely restaurant around. How Bingo's didn't sound exotic, and others might not know the kind of food that was served there. I tried to be as animated as possible, but all that was going through my mind was how I had started lying to Kelly too. Did it count as lying if I hid things from her?

That was another point that didn't matter. This wasn't how I wanted to start out my new life, on a foundation of lies and secrets. I could tell her now, but she would demand to know why I didn't tell her immediately. She warned and then begged me to stop agreeing to Megan's requests. I had also told her I had stopped but here I was thinking about how to take food home for Megan.

"What are you thinking about, Kev?"

I didn't want to talk about what I was thinking. Her again, I would have to lie.

"I'm not thinking about anything. I came here to relax but it isn't working."

Her face immediately turned into one of pity. She ran her fingers along the sides of my face, tracing the outlines of my jaw, drawing swirls and whorls. I liked it. I found it relaxing, somewhat.

"I'm so sorry. Work at the office must be stressing you out. It happens once in a while. I'm so sorry, Kev."

I nodded. I didn't know what to say. Maybe, it was best I did not say anything. Chances are, I would mess things up if I dared utter something untoward.

"Maybe I'll take the food home. I'm hungry, but I can't eat either."

"Oh, that's true. I'm sorry you feel so tired."

The apologies only made me feel more miserable. She loved me, and I repaid her with lies and deceit. The food was for Megan. That was the only reason I was here in the first place. I wondered when I became such a liar. Was I always this way, or it began when I started lying to Megan? I think that was the case. If I had never met Kelly, I didn't have had to lie to Megan in the first place.

But I now loved Kelly. Megan was trying to get in my head, and she was succeeding. This was what Kelly warned me about. Now, the roles were reversed, and I was now lying to Kelly.

I wondered what Megan was doing at this moment. Was she watching her favorite sitcom again? She had taken to drinking wine, and alcohol, trying not to think about their marriage that was headed for the rocks. Or she could be talking to her best friend. Megan told her everything. He wondered if they had talked about him if they had talked about her marriage. It was very likely as they told each other everything. Kevin had no problems with that. He was glad she had someone to talk to.

A memory of when they talked about this filtered into his head unprovoked.

"You don't talk to your friend anymore. Not like before."

I had said one night, a night after Kelly and I talked for an extended period at the gym. We hadn't started seeing each other yet, but I already knew I was in love with her.

"Bella is busy these days, and so am I. We haven't drifted apart or anything. We just haven't had time to catch up."

"Do you tell her everything?"

I was curious. Maybe Megan had noticed my irregular behavior and was relaying it all to her friend. I still wanted to be seen as a loving husband. Not one that had the hots for a coworker. I still wanted to be seen as the model lover, and Megan sure knew ways, many ways, to make me look good in front of others. I had to give her that.

"Not everything, everything. Of course, there's nothing I can't tell her, but a girl gotta has her secrets," She had said in a sing-song voice.

I laughed. I understood what she was talking about. We were once like each other, never trusting others completely, only ourselves. And here I was, telling a stranger everything about my marriage.

"And why would I need to tell anyone anything when you're right here?"

Guilt pangs tore through my chest as I drew her close. Even when I was cheating, there were times when he still managed to recapture the old times.

"Kevin. Kevin."

Kelly had been talking to me for a while now. She was tugging my shirt across the table, but I had been so deep in thought that I didn't notice.

"Hey. Sorry. I trailed off for a while."

I adjusted my shirt and made it to stand up. I had had enough and wanted to go home.

"Sit down, Kevin."

The harsh tone of her voice and the way she commanded me made more than a few heads turn in our direction. I sat down immediately. I was not too fond of confrontations, and it seemed Kelly was gearing up for one. My plan of action was to try and get her somewhere private. Kelly knew how to cause a scene easily, and I was sure she enjoyed it.

"Kelly. What is it? Before you talk, could we go out to the car? I don't want to stay here anymore."

She didn't have it

"Now you want to go? After I sacrificed my time following you here?"

I didn't ask her to come with me. But I didn't say that. I wanted to de-escalate as fast as possible. I reached out and held her hand. She was still angry, but she didn't pull away either.

"I haven't been feeling well. It's more emotional than physical, but that doesn't mean that it won't affect me sometimes. I'm really sorry. Tonight...no, the whole of today has mostly been a blur. I wanted to come here just to get away from everything, but it isn't helping. I'm really sorry."

I realized I was just going through the motions, saying whatever came to my head. I had become a very good liar lately. Kelly, in a way, had helped me to this point. Now I was using that weapon against her, and she didn't realize it.

"I'm sorry too, Kev," she said, looking into my eyes. I liked it when she did that. It made me feel loved, made me feel seen. She stretched out her hands over the table and held mine too. Then, I noticed the servers staring at me. The confused look in their eyes as they expected me to be with Megan, not a strange person.

Covertly, I disengaged our hands and led her outside. As we exited, I could see most of the tables and their occupants in the reflection of the glass doors. They looked happy and were engaged in conversation with their partners. We were once like that, Megan and I, but not anymore.

"I'll be going home now."

I had connected my order at the drive-in station of the restaurant and wanted to get home as soon as possible. Kelly looked a bit unhappy.

"Kev, are you okay? You were distracted throughout. Is anything the matter?"

I shook my head. I was at the door of my car, and her hands were around my waist. I looked over her shoulder, trying not to look her in the face and betray what I was thinking. Kelly could read my mind as easily as Megan. Or maybe I was too easy to read.

"Is it Megan? What is she doing these days? You haven't told me how the divorce is coming along."

This was it. I was going to lie again.

"She asked for some time before she signed it."

"What more time does she need again?"

I shrugged.

"Isn't there a way we could go around her? I'm tired of waiting, Kev. Let's get married soon. Aren't you tired too?"

I dragged her close, our faces almost touching. For a while, it's Megan, I see. But then the mirage cleared, and it was Kelly with her blue skirt suit and her hair packed into a bun, staring at me with her eyes that looked brown as the light of vehicles around shone into it.

I hugged her close. I was starting to discover many things about myself that I wasn't proud of.

"Let me take you home, Kel."

The easy conversations of when I began cheating on Megan were gone. For me, I loved her. Megan was messing with my head, just as Kelly had said. But I needed to see this through. I needed to get closure.

On my way home after dropping Kelly at her apartment, I thought about how she doted on me when I told her how I wasn't feeling too well. That was one area Megan never slacked, that was if she noticed. There was a particular time I had appendicitis and had to go in for surgery. It was hard, as I was in pain for a couple of weeks. Megan never left the hospital.

Okay, she must have left when I was out of it, but anytime I woke up, she was always by my side, forcing me to eat the food she prepared. She deserved closure too. I would go through with her requests and hope Kelly didn't find out.

Chapter 12

Megan

♥

Day Seven: Tuesday

I inspected the pink index card I had just written on, rereading the contents, wondering whether or not to put it out for Kevin.

He did get me dinner like I asked– *som tam* and the crab curry he knows I enjoy. I don't know if asking for this would be pushing it, but it's better if I ask for it all now because, in due time, I wouldn't be able to.

I was at my work table when his shadow suddenly blocked the light. Without a word, he placed the bag of takeout on my desk. Usually, I'd say something in protest– I was not too fond of food in my workspace– but I looked up and saw the pain in his eyes. He seemed to be hurting badly, but before I could ask him what was wrong, he hurried away with a mumbled, "Enjoy your dinner."

The food was still warm, so he must have just been heading back from Bingo's. Watching him like that hurt me, too, and I felt my eyes sting and water. And no, it wasn't from the curry.

This is why I wasn't sure I could go through with asking for my flowers.

He knew how much I loved forget-me-nots, and he usually got me those on my birthday. Except that in the past three years, I have had to remind him of my birthday, so asking for gifts was quite the stretch. A harried *happy birthday* was usually what I got.

Four years ago, he did not wish me either. I understand that he was pretty ill, so when my birthday came in the June of that year, birthdays weren't the first thing on our minds. I just wanted him alive and well. Many things happened within that four-year gap, and it beats me that I did not see the signs, nor did I see the markings on the wall until now, when it was already too late.

If my calculations were correct, he owed me three years' worth of forget-me-nots, but I'd be kind and remind him.

Even if it was just one stalk, a bouquet, or an entire garden of them, I wanted him to care enough to send me forget-me-nots. A beautiful pale blue, albeit painful reminder that I would eventually be forgotten, becoming mere fragments of his memories.

I knew these acts of desperation would do nothing to soothe the ache in my heart, but I did it all the same.

4. Remember the promise we made at Bingo's Diner on the eve of our second anniversary? I have not, for once, defaulted.

I bet you've loved every pair of cufflinks I've gotten you.

*I hope you've not forgotten forget-me-nots are my favorite? The florist isn't so **Fa**.*

~ Megan

I quit overthinking it and went to put it on the center table, where he would see it as he saw the others. Then, I went back to bed.

Later that morning, while I was preparing to leave for work, I noticed the card was still there. Shifted– so I know he had seen it– but it was still there.

Was he angry? Was he already tired of my incessant demands? Did he even see the point of this exercise? Has he finally grown tired of me?

Many similar thoughts in this regard swarmed my mind, even as I stood in the elevator with some other people headed to their respective working places.

It was hard to ignore the appreciative glances of some of them, though it was something I had to get used to while growing up. Then, it made me uncomfortable. Now, it was just plain tiresome, mostly ignored by me.

Slipping into my usual work-cheery self came quite quickly as I responded to greetings from coworkers, administrators, teachers, and even some students. I smiled through the workload, knowing that the school year would soon be over, and I was sure to turn in my resignation after the divorce proceedings. I savored the last bit of the Leyton high school pizzazz I was going to experience before I stopped working here.

I called Shanice during lunch, knowing she couldn't be far from her phone, Shanice being Shanice. A stay-at-home mom with a seven-figure earning husband, two kids, and a thriving female body positivity blog where she earns through influencing and brand adverts. She had *the life*. Everything that could go well was going well with her, and I feared she wouldn't understand me if I started to highlight the issues that led up to Kevin and me deciding to go on with the divorce. But I called anyway. She deserved to know.

"Shiny Shanice!"

"Yes, that's me... how have you been, baby girl? Tell me, Kevin couldn't keep his hands off you in that lingerie, could he?"

I let out a small laugh. "About that night...."

"Come on, spill the tea. Tell me all the juicy details."

Her excitement was palpable even through the phone. Poor Shanice. She probably thinks serious banging went down that night. The only banging that happened was that of my heart against my rib cage when Kevin told me he now felt for another woman. I didn't shed tears while in ecstasy, screaming Kevin's name. Rather, those tears fell when I realized I was now truly alone.

But how was I supposed to put this into words so Shanice would understand? I just had to say it as it was. Hopefully, she would not freak out too much.

"Um, actually, Kevin has filed for a divorce. He's been seeing someone else and...." I swallowed a lump that was fast forming in my throat and continued, "...he's happy with her."

There was a shocked silence on Shanice's end.

"Hello, are you there?"

"Yes. Yeah, I am. I just... it's just... have you guys tried talking things through?" The sadness that colored her voice brought tears to my eyes, but I fought to keep it restrained and not let it show in my voice.

"Um, yeah. Sort of. It seemed pretty straightforward to me. He doesn't want me anymore, which is pretty much about it."

"Wow, that's a lot. You know what? Let's have a girls' night out. Just us four. We'd come up with something, I promise."

My scalp suddenly felt itchy. "I don't know... I don't want to be a...burden to you guys."

I could almost see Shanice shaking her head. "Nonsense, dear. How does dinner at Bristles by seven sound?"

I agreed and tidied up my desk. The day was a bit slow, so I was even able to write two articles while in the Leyton office. The goal was to leave immediately after the school bell rang, find something to wear from my closet, and hit the road.

I settled for black slacks and a loose, blush-toned chiffon blouse. Low-block heels in black suede and a matching black purse were added to the ensemble. With setting spray and a few bobby pins to hold my hair in place, I put the finishing touches to my look with skin tint, mascara, cream blush, and of course, soft pink lipstick. They are said to make blue eyes pop. I was not exactly a pro in the makeup area, but I certainly knew my way around colors. And by *knowing my way*, I mean I stick mainly to neutrals, nudes, and beige tones. So much for shade.

I arrived relatively early at Bristles, the restaurant we were supposed to meet at by seven. I was there by 6:15, on purpose. I wanted to be there early so as to assuage my paranoid self that the girls weren't talking about me and my divorce before my arrival. Not like it was something they oft did, but it just is better to err on the side of caution, so they said.

The restaurant did not have a child-free policy like a few of the new ones that just sprung up, so there were a few families in the place at various stages of their meals.

A disgruntled father in the far right of the restaurant stood out to me. Their booth was decked in what seemed to be birthday decorations, and the six-year-old was a rather cute little boy who did not look very happy with the turn of events.

The manager seemed to be explaining something to him in hushed tones, but he didn't look like he was having any of it.

Just then, a young waitress appeared before me to take my order. For some reason, she reminded me of myself just a few years back when I worked quite a few shifts to make a living.

"I'm waiting for some friends. They would soon be here, and then, we'd order."

The lady nodded, but before she walked away, I quickly added, "Oh, and what is going on over there," gesturing with my jaw.

"Oh, that. The photographer who is supposed to cover the mini celebration as advertised in the celebration package wouldn't be showing up, and they had been looking forward to taking quite a few pictures, apparently."

I had put the camera in my bag to show the girls when explaining the part where Kevin now has to fulfill the promises from time past that divorce would absolve him from.

"I think I might be able to help. Tell your manager that," I said and brought out my camera pouch a tad too dramatically.

She nodded earnestly and bounded up to her manager. She whispered in his ear and pointed in my direction, and I gave a small wave.

He acknowledged me with a nod and then asked the father if he was okay with this new arrangement. He gave his consent. He just wanted to get it all over with.

I briskly walked over to the man, his son, and the two other adults that flanked the birthday boy. On closer inspection, he had a little sister at his side. *So cute.*

I felt a bit self-conscious, but I ignored the feeling and introduced myself.

"Good evening. I couldn't help but notice the birthday boy here."

"Aww, thank you. Emma here says you're a photographer."

I nodded in the affirmative. "Nothing too grand, but I sure do take decent pictures."

"Just that is enough. I just want him to have a good enough birthday celebration."

I swung into action immediately, wondering where I found the funny bone to make everyone laugh as often as I did. It was necessary so that I could capture the most genuine smiles from the needed angles. I needed the emotions raw, the moments real, the smiles unforced. Chuck needed the best birthday ever, and I was going to be part of the forces of the universe that would give him that.

The whole picture-taking session did not take so long, as I was done in about thirty-five minutes. I showed him the pictures I had taken, and he looked genuinely impressed.

"Wow, thank you so much. So, how much do I pay you now?" he asked, his face all aglow from a lot of smiling.

"Consider it my gift to the birthday boy. Now, how to send you the pictures... I could send the pictures to your email as soon as I get home?"

"Yes. Yes, please. Thank you so very much. You're so kind."

He went ahead to scribble his mail on a serviette. While he was writing, I spotted Shanice, Andrea, and Tori at a corner booth. Tori's platinum blonde hair was like a neon sign in this sea of dark-haired people, so it was very easy to spot them.

Tori looked like she was going to come over, but Andrea held her back. I instantly wished the man would write faster, so I didn't have to keep them waiting any longer. He looked like he was going to make small talk, so I quickly gestured toward my table and said I had people waiting for me.

As soon as I collected the serviette he scribbled his mail on, I hurried over to my friends, excited about the adventure I had just had.

If they were going to talk about the divorce, they did not bother to bring it up anymore. Broaching that dreadful topic while I relayed the exciting night's events wasn't very tactful, so I was grateful they let me be happy in peace. They instead just offered words of encouragement and support, refusing to mention the fact that I was going through a divorce.

Candace was running late. She met us midway through our dessert. We teased her about her lateness. The yellow and orange flouncy dress she wore draped nicely about her plump frame, while her black shoes and accessories gave her attire a tasteful finish.

"If it isn't Queen Candace gracing us with her presence," Andrea casually said before burying a Buffalo wing in her mouth. How she knew Candace was the one coming surprised me because Andrea's back was to the door.

"Hey...Babies. I'm sorry. I had to find Ethan a babysitter at the last minute."

Shanice tutted. "You should just have brought him along. I've missed him."

Half the time, my mouth was stuffed full of food, so talking was not exactly high on my priorities. My appetite also seemed to be raging at the moment, unlike the dry disinterest that had plagued my eating habits for the past few days.

It was just so refreshing to hang out with the girls after quite a while. The manager sent a platter of bite-sized chops to our table, probably as a thank-you for my helping with the photographs. We were full, but we kept on eating.

"Looks like your hobby is paying off! Please take more pictures so that we can get more free food!" Tori teased me while helping herself to a spring roll.

"Don't be ridiculous! You want to send fast food joints out of business?"

It was cute seeing Chuck and his little sister, Lily, wave at me while leaving the restaurant to be on their way home. It felt somewhat fulfilling to be able to help random strangers.

When I stumbled out of the elevator in my apartment building at 9:22 pm, the worries from this morning came rushing back to me.

Is he back? Or has he packed his things and left my demanding miserable self and me? Did he even get the point of these notes?

My worry heightened when I opened the door, and I noticed the card was still where it was, slant like I left it this morning and when I came home to change.

I sighed. *This one was a failure, then.* I went to his room to be sure he had even come home at all.

I opened the door with a crack. His funny self had fallen asleep in his towel, exposing his slightly hairy thigh. It was amusing to see him like that, but I immediately felt guilty. I wasn't supposed to be seeing him like that. It felt like I was an intruder, and I wouldn't say I liked the feeling at all, so I closed the door as quietly as possible.

My laptop was in the living room, so I proceeded to send the man his pictures, using *'Happy Birthday, Chuck!'* as the subject of the mail. His reply was nearly instantaneous, like he was waiting for my email to be delivered. His reply:

I would have personally called you to thank you for your kindness, but I understand that it's late. These are the best pictures of my family someone has ever taken. Every emotion at the right time was captured in them. And you didn't even let me pay you too. I hope you got the platter of chops I paid for, and it's the least I could do.

Thank you,

Adam (Chuck's Dad)

I returned to my room and planned to crawl into bed after replying to that email with a generic "thank you," but what I saw completely knocked me off balance.

There was a large bouquet of forget-me-nots surrounded by white roses with a card lodged among the petals.

I can never forget that. Even our splitting up wouldn't rob me of those memories.

I'm sorry for all your birthdays that I missed... And for the ones coming up that I will miss.

~ Kevin

Why did I choose to put myself through this torture, you may ask? Even I did not know why exactly. I thought I knew, but as it stands, I'm not quite sure of what I know anymore.

The promises of yesteryears, can today fulfill them? Or is it an exercise in futility?

Chapter 13

Kevin

♥

Day Nine: Thursday

Her next request involved the two of us. The first of her requests did.

5. Remember, we always thought going to cinemas was generic, but then when it was a Tom Cruise movie, we just had to see it.

*It was nice. We went, we **So** and I ate your popcorn while you concentrated on the movie. You promised to take your revenge.*

Well, now's your chance. The sequel to that
movie is showing soon. This weekend, maybe?

~ *Megan*

I remembered the movie. Tom Cruise was fantastic. He was a living legend, one of a kind. I had watched all of his movies before this one. I was planning to go with Kelly, but it seemed Megan had other plans. Kelly had been looking forward to it and had reminded me in the office yesterday.

I had to cancel. I was going to be with Kelly for the rest of my life while Megan and I would soon be divorced. Besides, I could see she needed this for herself, for both of us. We needed closure. I had to get the tickets online, but first of all, I had to cancel with Kelly and give her a plausible excuse.

Last time at Bingo's, I had lied to her that I wasn't feeling too good. But I couldn't continue to say that every time. I had to come up with something even better before I reached the office. It seemed Megan had gone to the gym once again. I took my briefcases and started to leave for the office. As I walked out, I stopped to look at myself in the mirror in our bedroom.

I remembered when she found out about Kelly, and this was the same outfit I had on. Much had changed since that time. A lot. But it all started that night. The night of our anniversary. Despite that, the truth remained. Despite my reluctance to follow through with her requests, despite Kelly's instructions not to fall victim to Megan's alleged mind games, I was starting to look forward to the requests she made. I looked forward to taking her to see the movie.

Kelly was waiting for me at the door to my office. She had been doing that a lot these days. I didn't know if she was purely expecting me and couldn't wait for me to show up or if she was wondering if I wouldn't show up. Maybe Megan had finally convinced me to forget the divorce and resign from work so I wouldn't see her again.

"Kev."

She rarely said hello.

"Kel. Waiting on me again this morning?"

I opened my door and went in. She followed. I heard the muffled sound of her heels on the rug in my office. She was wearing her usual skirt suit, only this time, it was black, and the skirt was more than a bit short.

"Nice skirt," I said after I sat down. She burst out laughing, her perfect dentition showing. It had been a long time since I saw her laugh like that.

She came and sat in my lap, the skirt riding further up her thigh. Her eyes were bright, and she was happy.

"I thought about you while choosing my outfit for today. So I decided to go wild. What do you think?"

For an answer, I tilted her face and kissed her. She returned the gesture with equal enthusiasm. But after a few seconds, she pulled away and sat on the table.

"So I had an idea yesterday after we left. What would you say to a romantic getaway?" she queried. I raised an eyebrow and swept my hands over my table. There was a lot of paperwork that wasn't done. My personal life was getting in the way of my business.

But that wasn't what I was thinking about too. Not entirely. I had purchased the movie tickets for Megan and me. I was yet to form an excuse that would be believable. But if there was ever a time to lie, it was now. However, Kelly was talking.

"Come on; you know you can easily postpone till next week. Or would you work over the weekend or spend time with me?"

When she put it that way, it was hard to say anything other than what she wanted. I had to go broke. I had already tried the ever-reliant "I'm busy" excuse, and it didn't work. There was another angle I could pursue, but my mind was still working out the kinks.

"Plus, we still have our movie. From here, we could go to the hotel room I paid for. Just me and you, Kevin, away from Megan and everything else."

It was tempting.

"I should have told you since. Remember the Thai restaurant we went to when I told you I wasn't feeling too well?"

She looked confused.

"Yes, I remember. What has that got to do with anything?'

It was now or never.

"My mother. She had been diagnosed with Alzheimer's. So I have to see her. I've been pushing it away because I didn't want to see her like that, but she has irrationally requested to see me this weekend."

Kelly was immediately apologetic.

"I'm so sorry, Kev. There was no way I could have known all these. I knew you were deep in thought and distracted that day, but there was no way I could have known. I'm sorry," she kept repeating, and my conscience continued to send me painfully stinging jabs.

"It's okay. No need to apologize. It isn't your fault. It's nobody's. I'm going there, so...raincheck on the movie?"

She looked crestfallen.

"It wasn't only the movie. I had booked a room, Kev," she replied quietly.

"I'm sorry, Kel. I hope you understand. My hands are tied. I'll make it up to you. I promise."

She nodded and made to leave my office. I had expected her to stay longer, but I could see that she was utterly disappointed. My conscience repeated the same stabbing sequence.

"Wait, can't I come with you?"

What?

"I don't understand."

"You always said you wanted me to come and meet your mom. This is as good a time as any, Kev."

I was lost for words. But Kelly wasn't.

"Do you think she'll like me? What should I get her?"

"Slow down." But she wasn't listening anymore. I could hear the excitement in her voice. I should have stuck with the truth. Now she was spiraling into a rabbit hole. I could bet she had already started to imagine herself greeting my parents and wondering how and if they would accept her. Whether she would be expected to bring gifts or just bring herself. I could see the wheels turning in her head, the light bulb flicking on and off.

"But she has met Megan, hasn't she? How would that look, you bringing another woman to meet your family? Have you told any of them about me or your problems with Megan?"

"Kelly." I almost shouted, but it got her attention.

"My mom loves Megan, and now she has been diagnosed with Alzheimer's. I don't think taking another woman to meet her right now is a good idea."

She made to say something and stopped herself.

"Say what you're thinking, Kel."

"Are you going with Megan?"

"No, I'm not."

"Does she know?" she inquired.

"About?" I was getting close to my wit's end.

"Come on, your mum. What else are we talking about?"

We weren't talking now. We were very close to a fight. Kelly was jealous or suspicious. I didn't know which one it was.

"No, she doesn't know. You're the first person I'm telling. No one else knows."

She backed down.

"I'm sorry. I... looked forward to spending time with you. I've been really bored these days, and you've been busy with work. So I planned all of it and wanted us to hang out."

She sounded like a high school teenager who was told by her crush that he wouldn't be able to go on a date with her because he was busy. She sounded petty and entitled. As far as she knew, I was going to see my mother, who was sick, and here she was, asking if I was going with Megan.

"I have to go see my mum, Kelly. I'm sorry if you're upset, but it is what it is. I'll see you later." I told her dismissively. She exited without any further ado. I didn't know what was going on in her mind. I wasn't even sure I wanted to know.

The movie was impressive. It wasn't a Tom Cruise movie, after all. The tickets to that were sold out by the time I got there after work. I could have ordered online, but I completely forgot. The paperwork I had been dodging turned out to be more than I thought, and I tried to do as much as possible before I went home. The only movie showing at the cinema was a romantic comedy.

I didn't want to get the tickets at first, not wanting to send the wrong impression. But I had no choice. As much as I was starting to enjoy the requests, I wanted them to be over as soon as possible. So, I bought the tickets.

Chapter 14

Kevin

♥

Day Eleven: Saturday

The movie was slated for Saturday around 4 pm. When it was almost time for us to get going, I went to remind her to get dressed. I half-expected her to be behind her laptop, typing away, oblivious to how much time had passed. But she was in the room dressing. It looks like this outing mattered to her, somehow. I didn't want to intrude and decided to wait for her to come out on her own accord.

Meanwhile, Kelly was breaking our rule of not sending texts when we were away from each other. Granted, the rule was made when we didn't want Megan to find out when I didn't want Megan to find out about my clandestine activities, and right now, she already knew. So there was no reason not to, and in addition, Kelly didn't care whether Megan found out or not in the first place.

This had me questioning a lot—her stance. If my opinion mattered, I shook the thoughts out of my head. Why couldn't Kelly send me a text or even call? She missed me and wanted to talk to me. That was another thing Megan rarely did. She had her good days, but her bad days were worse than anything I could imagine.

Moreover, she thought I was with my mother. No one would blame her if she called to check up on me.

Kelly: How is she?

Me: She is not as bad as we expected. :)

Kelly: That's good. When will you be back?

Me: I don't know yet. Soon, I hope. Can't wait to see you, Kel.

I didn't know if I wrote that because it was true, because I wanted it to be true or if that was what she wanted to hear.

Kelly: Same here, Kev. Come back soon.

I heard a cough. It was Megan, and she was beautiful. She wore a white top and jeans skirt, which was how she dressed when we met. Something so casual, yet she pulled it off with ease. Now, she was watching the movie with renewed vigor. My popcorn was almost halved, and I could have sworn that I didn't eat up to half. And unless my pack was leaking, the only excuse was that Megan had been pilfering when I wasn't looking.

It had been years since we last came to a cinema. I loved the action, while she only wanted to watch movies that involved romance. So, we came to a compromise. We would be watching two movies anytime we were here.

"Unwind, Kevin. You're not at work anymore. Why aren't you watching?"

I laughed. If only she knew about the argument Kelly and I had regarding this particular topic. But I couldn't deny the fact that I was having a good time. The movie wasn't as bad as I thought. It would be over soon but it was worth watching.

Then like magic, Megan brought two tickets out of her bag. It was for the sold-out Tom Cruise movie I forgot to order tickets for. *How thoughtful!* The gesture did take me by surprise, truth be told.

"Why did you do that?" I asked her.

It was her turn to laugh.

"You keep forgetting that I know you very well. You would be too lazy to purchase tickets for more than one movie. I know your work, and I thought this would be a good way for you to relax."

I was shocked and glad at the same time. It was nice knowing that someone was thinking about you. I had missed this. I didn't want this feeling to end. Meanwhile, Kelly kept calling as I wasn't replying to her texts.

Juggling the past and the future sure is stressful.

Chapter 15

Megan

♥

Day Eleven: Saturday

At first, I was sure I had overstepped my bounds with my last request. Willing to live with the consequences of my rather bold actions, I did not begin dressing up for the movie outing until I heard the elevator bell ding. Even at that, I did not know what to wear exactly.

Since the goal was to remind him of the good times– I'd like to believe that was the reason for my going through all this trouble– I opted for an outfit that I felt was going to be for him, most nostalgic, though I doubted he would even remember.

A frilly white top and a blue denim button-up skirt that stopped before my knee.

I think he did. I don't know. I can't tell. It was hard trying to figure him out these days. The movies we saw were great, and that was about it. Something in me wondered if there would be...more somewhere, somehow. I guess that was just the blindly-optimistic side of me hoping for some sort of respite.

Sleep was far from my eyes these days, and the reason was not far-fetched. I lay in bed, staring at the white bleakness of the ceiling.

I remember trying to be so perfect for him in the latter days of our courtship. He was the one person I had ever imagined spending the great of my life with, and I just could not afford to mess it up.

I was so scared of messing things up for quite a long time– till I met his mother.

Seven Years Ago...

The minute I met her, I knew I had signed up for a lifetime's worth of trouble, but I was already too invested. The disapproving look that was tossed in my direction when she saw I was the one in the driver's seat instead of her precious son was enough to send any woman cowering– but not me.

I very well noted that my greetings were not replied and when I asked where I could drop the fresh flowers I got her, she merely gestured to the kitchen, too busy fussing over her baby. Marigolds and lilies that I only got with my money just because Kevin said she loved them. I found an empty vase and began putting them in, taking my sweet time because I was still trying to process the far-from-warm reception I had just got.

She made no effort to whisper as she asked her son, "Is that the one you told me about? Hmmph! She barely has any flesh on her." I couldn't hear Kevin's response, but I strongly doubt he said anything to correct her.

Her pitchy voice came on again. "Don't you like Cathy, Mrs. Laurent's daughter? I can get you introduced to her at the next Hall meeting...you'd be coming, right?"

The said Hall Meeting was on a Thursday, and Kevin and I had made plans, so naturally, I expected him to decline. He didn't. He then went on to tell me that he did not want to disappoint her, so he canceled our plans.

During the dinner, his mum asked me to tell her about myself, all smiley and stuff. I must admit, I must have let down my guard so much that I didn't see through her baits and traps.

"So, Marissa, tell me about yourself."

I nearly choked on the saltless turkey piece I had just put it in my mouth. Not just because of the bland taste– though I suspect strongly that it was a contributing factor– but how does anyone get Megan wrong? It had to be on purpose because, let's face it, she was not that old, nor did she have any memory-impairing disease. I forced myself to swallow and sipped the orange juice that was set before me to rid my mouth of that stuff before I spoke.

"It's Megan, ma'am. I'm twenty-three, originally from Charleston, South Carolina, and moved here when I got into college."

"Looks like Kevin has copped himself a southern belle!" she said and laughed. A laugh I wasn't sure was nice or mocking.

"So, you went to college. What do you do for a living?"

It felt like an interview of sorts. One that determined the next phase of my life. *I'm a good person. She just has to like me.*

"I'm expecting feedback from a few firms, but in the meantime, I do freelance writing."

She leveled me with a blank look. "So...you have no job." She and her son shared a look. She sipped the cabernet sauvignon that sat in her glass. "Your parents are still back South? Your siblings? How's your family like?"

"Just my Mom, really. I didn't grow up with a dad or anything. It's always just been my mum and I."

Her next words were one of the cruelest things I've ever had spoken to me up to that point. "Raised by a single mother? I wonder what kind of family values you have. Can you even keep a man? You know, seeing as you had no example to learn from...."

Kevin drawled out a weak "Mum..." and then joined his mother laughing.

That visit was, needless to say, one of the most embarrassing events of my life. The unannounced Saturday visits she paid us after we got married annoyed me so much, but Kevin never seemed to understand what used to piss me off. What broke the straw on the camel's back for me was the day she popped by with a casserole as was her custom and concluded that because there was no pre-cooked dinner in the fridge, I was a 'bad wife who had had no good example and could not treat a man right.'

It is funny to recall how when Kevin had to be hospitalized and had surgery for appendicitis, and she visited only once and never helped me take care of the baby she claimed to love so much. I remember him crying and saying his mother was so wrong about me that he would tell her that to her face once he was okay. He still has not.

I was the bad wife, yet I stayed. No matter what I did, I was still the bad wife to her since I was not Cathy, her preferred candidate.

So, when I stared at the blank index card, wanting to leave a note for Kevin, I knew just what to ask for.

6. Remember my first visit with you to your Mom's? You might not remember what went down that day, but there were statements along the lines of me not knowing 'how to treat a man right'.

Also, do you remember when you promised after your surgery that you'd set things straight with her to her face?

Cal-La today. Tell her she was wrong about me.

~ Megan

Satisfied with what I had written, I placed it on the center table, knowing very well that he'd see it on his way out. I went on to have a popcorn-fueled sleep and a fuzzy dream of warm Bali skies and tropical fruits. A weird but pleasant dream, nonetheless.

Later the following day, as I waited for my toast to brown a little more, my phone rang, startling me. No one called me these days. I once checked if my phone had its Do Not Disturb feature on cause my phone does not ring with calls anymore.

The call was coming from an unsaved number. The only thing I could tell was that it wasn't a foreign number. I picked up on the second ring.

"Hello. Good morning. Am I on to Ms. Megan Stewart?"

Shocking. Who knows me?

"Hello. Good morning. Yeah, who am I on to, please?"

A slight chuckle from the other end greeted my ears. "I don't know if you remember the family you took pictures of at Bristles the other day. It was Chuck's birthday?"

I laughed. *How did he get my number?* "Ah, yeah, I remember. How's the little lad? And Lily?"

"They're fine, thanks for asking. I did a lot of scouring to get your number, as I have something of importance I was hoping to discuss with you."

"How may I help you? I'm all ears." I went back to my toast which was now more than slightly brown. I doused the slices in butter and pulled a stool to sit at the kitchen counter while listening to what the man had to say.

"I'm Adam Harrison, CEO of Shlux... I don't know if you're familiar with our operations...."

Shlux. Shlux. Why does that sound so familiar? I set the toast I had in my hand down and quickly searched them on Google. It turns out they were a multinational corporation. A glance through their some told me that they were bigshots in the hospitality business.

"...but we want to do a promotion on our luxury travel destinations with a touch that is more personal-oriented than scripted. It would require a sort of, uh, nomadic photographer. I don't know if you'd be open to traveling the world, documenting your travels in images as part of the exposition."

"Wow." My head spaced out for a minute or two.

"I'd understand if you have a lot of engagements. I mean... that would be understandable. I'd love it if you could think about it."

"This is shocking...."

"The board was also impressed with the pictures you took at Chuck's birthday, and when the publicity team said they did not want a celebrity photographer, you instantly came to mind, and I put you forward."

"That's so nice of you, Adam. I really wasn't expecting this. I do photography as a hobby and nothing serious. Are you sure you want me, though?"

He laughed. He had this easiness about him, the simplicity that he had always borne since their first meeting till now.

"I know what I want. And it's you. As Shlux's travel photographer, of course. Do you mind coming to the office so we can talk about it properly? Is today done for you?"

I ran my schedule through my head and realized nothing was pressing.

"I should be able to drop by at 1 pm. Could you please mail me the office address?"

I heard a clap from his end, meaning he was using the device hands-free. It was likely connected to a loudspeaker or headphones. The board might as well have been listening in.

"Splendid then. Looking forward to seeing you by 1 pm."

The call ended. I was excited and so worked up that I abandoned the toast. The overly simple dress I planned to wear to work today just wouldn't cut it.

I returned to my closet, selected a navy pantsuit and a beige cami, and wore those instead.

As I boarded the taxi that was to drop me at the entrance of Leyton High, I set the alarm for 12:45 pm. I did not plan to be late for the meeting at all.

Being a nomad with a camera has never been on my life plans, but the universe sure has funny ways of tossing these things at you. What I did not know yet, though, was whether or not I was going to hold on to what was thrown at me.

Shlux's head office was somewhere in Edgewater, and locating it was no problem at all. I got into their posh lobby at 12:58 pm. I know because I was nervously checking the time throughout the thirteen-minute-long journey.

The extra politeness when I gave my name to the receptionist certainly did not escape my notice, and I could only chuckle to myself in the elevator as I wondered why that sort of to was common among people.

"You're welcome, Megan." He checked his watch. "And right on time, too. A woman of her word, I see."

"Hello, Adam. Glad to be here."

He gestured me towards one of the plush seats before his glass and chrome desk, so easily settling in the executive chair that made him look larger than life. Even the office looked larger than life. Shiny glass and tasteful décor. The place screamed class in volumes that left me wondering if I was below the poverty line.

"So, let me delve right into it."

I nodded and brought out a pen and a small notepad to jot down important things he might have to say. I guess my action amused him a little because he chuckled. The unassuming man I met at Bristles the other day now seemed somewhat intimidating. Not cold or standoffish, but now knowing him as an important figure, it became hard to reconcile the simple t-shirt-wearing Adam as the same person as the imposing CEO Adam that now sat before me.

"Shlux is currently one of the largest names in the hospitality business industry, and we're seeking to expand even more. We've previously served only the elite, but now we want to bring the world-class standard to the common man."

I nodded, understanding him, but I could not help but wonder about the strategy to be used to achieve this lofty goal he had just stated.

"Yeah, so, my new initiative will help to connect culturally diverse people across the globe and bring them closer," he said and handed me a brochure showing different luxury destinations. The graphics design was really good, but there was a kind of detachment from the attached photos that made it all look plastic. Now, I understood what he was saying over the phone.

"I need people to understand that there is real fun in traveling, and there's a package for every pocket size. There's a lot more that could be experienced in these places, and we need this message circulated as widely as possible. Images leave a strong impact on people...you'd know this better than anyone else."

I gave a generic response that even I can't remember at the moment. It sounded like fun and a lot of work...but it sounded pretty exciting too.

"To spread this message, this company seeks someone who understands people's emotions and has a gift to bring the best sides of a place to the fore."

I smiled when I heard him say that. *Me? Understand emotions?* Well, if I did, my husband would not have served me divorce papers– I'd have noticed the rift that built up for four years.

"The pictures of my family you took really impressed me and showed a certain softness about us that I hadn't seen captured before. It's not flattery, but you're a great photographer, and our message needs the kind of raw honesty you bring to the table... Do you consider working for us?"

I went quiet for a bit, still struggling to come to terms with the reality of the situation.

"Oh, the company will cover the travel expenses, transport, and lodging. Remuneration can be negotiated. We're offering between 100,000 and 150,000 dollars per annum. We could work out the nitty-gritty of the contract as soon as you give your word."

It was all too much to take in. My mouth went dry as I fumbled to look for words.

"Okay, um, it's a great offer. Really, it is, but do you mind if I send a response via mail? I'd have to put things in order first...."

He nodded, his eyes crinkling in a smile. *Putting things in order...what things, even?* I shook my head. After these two and a half days, Kevin will be out of my life. Sure, being a travel photographer never occurred to me as a viable career choice, but I would need ample distraction from the sob story that was now my life.

With a fierceness that stunned me, I looked the CEO of Shlux in the eye and said, "I'd take the offer."

At last, thanks to this, I can see the world without restraints.

Chapter 16

Kevin

♥

Day Thirteen: Monday

7. Remember how we first met? Valentine's Day and Donuts?

*I don't think I've ever had better-tasting donuts **Ti** ll date.*

Would you get me donuts with my favorite filling from that drive-through?

~ Megan

I t was quite simple this time. A donut from where she worked when she was a student. The place where we first met. She would never let me rest, always telling me about how she always wanted to go back and see how the place was. But this time, it was apparent what she was trying to get me to do. Remember how we first met? If I was being honest, I had expected her to include this in one of her notes before now. Maybe she was saving the best for one of the last. It was also at the back of my mind that the fourteen days before the divorce agreement would soon be over. Kelly had also been reminding me of this fact. But I knew, I had known for a while now, known that I had been enjoying the notes she had been sending to me.

Megan had been working at a donut shop while she was at college. I didn't notice her at all. I always passed through the drive-through section on my way to work when I was still an intern. I didn't know who she was going to be at that time. We were still strangers to each other then. But the first day I saw her, I truly saw her, and I will never forget it.

Seven Years Ago...

Once again, I was getting late and in a hurry. I had to assist the manager with a presentation to the executives. I had been warned numerous times to desist from this habit, and sometimes I succeeded, but today was not one of those days.

"Good morning. What would you like today?"

It was Megan. I saw the tag on her shirt, a pink and flowery shirt with *Barry's Place* in italics written all over too.

"Good morning. I would like a jelly donut with a cup of coffee," I replied and then turned to my dash to take my wallet.

It wasn't there. I didn't think much about it. I proceeded to move to my pockets to search for some change to purchase what I had ordered. I always had some spare change in my pockets that had rescued me from some situations in which I managed to find myself—situations just like this. I came up with nothing. I could feel the blood rush to my face.

"Here are the donuts you ordered, sir."

I looked at her in embarrassment.

"I'm sorry, I'm going to have to cancel that. Left my wallet at home."

"Oh. I..."

"You can't return an order? Can I pay on my way back? You can keep the donuts too."

I was flinging options left and right, wanting to get out of there as soon as possible. Other drivers behind me shared the same sentiment as they honked and shouted at me to get a move on.

"You can talk to the pretty waitress later. You're wasting our time here, man," someone had shouted.

The shouts from others were only increasing my embarrassment. I watched her tilt her head to the side.

"Well, I've seen you here a couple of times. You can take the donuts and pay tomorrow."

I was taken aback.

"No, I can't do that."

"Why? You buy here every morning, and you better go before the others start a riot. And between you and me, they probably can. So you better hurry."

I would have thanked her more than I eventually did, but I could already see a particularly hefty guy coming out of his car. I zoomed off immediately. I promised myself I would be back in the evening no matter what. I would surprise her. I didn't usually take that route on my way back as the traffic was typically hectic. I didn't make it, and I was too tired even to drive that long.

The following morning, I was there early before the morning rush, and I found her waiting for customers to show up. It was then I truly saw her. The man in the car behind me yesterday wasn't wrong. She was beautiful. She had that raven black hair that I lived in, woman. As I approached her, she looked back and saw me. A smile lit up her face.

"Good morning," I said, maybe a bit too eagerly. My hand was already in my pocket. This time, I made sure I had change and brought my wallet. It wouldn't have looked good if I said I had forgotten my wallet again.

"Hey. Back early today."

She looked behind my car in mock alarm, "And look, it looks like the troublemakers aren't here yet. So you have time."

"Time for?" I was smiling. Who wouldn't, in the face of such radiance? I thought she wanted to talk to me for a while, with the reference she made to time being plenty.

"Your buttons aren't in the right order," she replied, pointing at my shirt.

I looked down in horror and saw what she meant. My buttons were not arranged properly, and the first two were not fastened. I groaned inwardly. I had tried my best to ensure I was early enough, and now I wasn't appropriately dressed. I thought this wasn't the type of impression I wanted to make, as I dressed up appropriately, using my rearview mirror.

"Thank you very much. Good thing I didn't appear in the office looking like this. I didn't even notice."

She smiled again, looking at the menu next to the drive-through window. I counted the money I owed from yesterday and gave it to her.

"Thank you," she said in a singsong voice.

Now that I had paid, I usually would have ordered for my usual donuts and been on my way immediately, but I wanted to talk to her. She was intriguing to me all of a sudden. She didn't speak much, but I could see that a lot was going on in her head.

I had many questions I wanted to ask. Did she live around? Was this a full-time job for her? Many students were working around the area in various small establishments. Was she one of them? I couldn't guess her age from her appearance alone.

"So, what's your favorite donut? I'd like to try something new today. And don't say your favorite is the one I normally order."

She rolled her eyes and smiled again. I started feeling good.

"Well, I don't know if you'll like it too, but I prefer strawberry. If we're being honest, I don't know how anybody can stand chocolate in their donuts."

It was my turn to laugh. She had a sense of humor. I used to order chocolate donuts once upon a time, mostly on days when I was feeling down.

"Let's see how strawberry goes then. Two, please."

I watched her disappear behind the counter, preparing my order. This was the chance I had. I didn't know if she had someone already. Mostly, it was a spur-of-the-moment decision. Okay, maybe not so hasty. It had occurred to me sometime during the night. It seemed like a bad idea at the time. It still seemed like a bad idea and very cliché, hitting on the pretty waitress. The words of that man echoed in my ears again. I didn't care this time, and I wrote what I wanted on a piece of paper.

She came back and announced to me, "Well, you're to pay for only one donut." She handed both to me, packed separately.

"Why?"

"Oh. Valentine's Day special and all that. I was supposed to tell you it was a buy-one-get-one-free promo and all that. It slipped my mind."

She grimaced. "Sorry."

I was now rethinking my letter. From the way she talked, it was obvious she didn't care much about Valentine's day. This was common among single people, but it didn't mean she wasn't in a relationship either. Also, it changed how I thought she was going to view what I wrote. Now, my note might be greeted with a bit of skepticism and, if I was lucky, plain indifference.

"You have something against Valentine's Day?"

I had only five minutes before rush hour started. I already saw her glance at her watch covertly. I pretended not to notice.

"Not really. I'm just floating. Neither here nor there."

"I understand."

I didn't.

"Could I get extra napkins, please?"

"No problem." She replied as she went back in.

This was my chance. I stuck the note on one of the donut packs and promptly made my way out of there. I saw the now-familiar Toyota Camry belonging to the man who had shouted at me the day before.

Now, as I drove away, there were a couple of things that ran through my mind. I didn't want to ponder on any of them long enough to regret my decision. But as I saw her, in my rearview, pick up the note I had left and smile, I knew it wasn't such a bad idea after all. I didn't want her to think I was being charitable. I wanted her to see it as a gift. That was why my note read:

Happy Valentine's Day.

~Kevin

I had wanted to add more, thanking her for yesterday and hoping we could become friends later on. But I didn't go through with it. I will see her again tomorrow. At least now she knew my name even though she never asked.

The next day, I made sure my buttons were done this time, and I steeled myself for any backlash from the note I left, if there was any. I highly doubted there would be any, but it didn't hurt to prepare. However, when I got to the drive-through window, she wasn't there. There was a guy there taking orders already. This time, the Camry was there before me. I had to turn right around and go in through the front door. The car park in front of *Barry's Place* was almost filled at this time of the day. It made sense that they had a drive-through section to cater to more of their customers.

I didn't know if she would be in. Maybe today was her off day, or she was down with the flu. But all those theories were immediately dashed as I saw her attending to customers inside. Her face lit up with a smile when she saw me standing by the door. She motioned to a table for me to get seated. I walked over to where she told me, but before I could get there, I heard a customer yelling.

"What is this? What the hell is this?"

He spoke in an Irish accent. He wore biker clothes and had a body covered in tattoos.

"I'm sorry. How can I help you?"

I noticed the tremor in her voice.

"How can you help me? I just drank the worst coffee I have ever tasted in my life. You didn't put any whiskey. I specifically asked for a shot of whiskey in the coffee."

"I'm sorry. There is no...whiskey. I mean, we don't serve alcohol at *Barry's.*"

He was dangerously close to her. A mug filled with hot coffee was being brandished, the dangerously hot contents spilling all over the tiled floor. Other customers were having their meals looked on, and the other waitress on duty had disappeared into the backroom, probably to get the manager. I wondered if he was so dead that he couldn't hear the ruckus happening in his establishment.

"Excuse me, sir. You heard..."

I didn't know if he somehow used the hand holding the coffee or if he used the other. I just knew that I saw a fist flying straight for my jaw. I saw black stars dancing, and the next thing I knew, I was headed for a table involuntarily. Luckily for me, there were no occupants, so I steadied myself on a chair and sat down. I couldn't speak, and the stars refused to return to their solar system. I wasn't eating any donuts that day, that was for sure.

I heard someone speak with authority.

"That's it—full-on assault. I'm calling the police. Get out of here now."

I saw a black mass pass by my side menacingly. He glanced at me, chuckled, and walked away.

Thinking about it now, I realized the punch hurt me way more than I cared to admit to Megan when she gave me a pack of ice trying to help with the injury.

"You don't have to worry. I'm fine. I've received worse."

She smiled that smile I was now familiar with.

"I'm sure you have."

I couldn't help it. We both burst out laughing.

"Thank you... for standing up for me."

I felt my shoulders raise a notch higher than their normal position.

"So, how can I make it up to you?"

Here was my chance.

"I don't know. Maybe a date?"

It was an incredible story, one of those you will never forget. But as I drove into that same drive-through many years later, I tried to look at it from her perspective. I was her knight in shining armor. The way I stood up to the Black Biker, as we've called him, I was proud of myself. Here's this real asshole who's treated her like garbage and ruined her self-esteem, but then suddenly, someone's there, standing up for her. Me. She loved me from then on, she once revealed. How would it feel knowing that your knight in shining armor doesn't want you anymore?

Maybe I wasn't really a knight. I was a liar, even below garbage. Garbage didn't lie, and garbage didn't hide, didn't break your heart. I did all those. I wasn't any knight. I was the lowest of the low, less than garbage.

I got her a strawberry donut and knew this time I should leave a note like I did all those years. Just like then, I had many things I needed to say, a lot of things I wanted her to know. Finally, I settled on a simple sentence.

I'm sorry.

~Kevin

But before I got home, I picked up the phone and called my mother. There was one other request that I hadn't gone through with.

"Hey, Mum."

It had been a long time since I had called her.

"Kevin? I have to say, this is a surprise."

She was always straight to the point. It hadn't earned her many friends, but that was what I was looking for.

"How are things with Megan? How is she?"

I smiled. I didn't think she cared that much about what happened to Megan.

"I called to tell you how wrong you were about her."

There was silence on her end.

"Kevin?"

And all of a sudden, I couldn't hold back anymore. I think that was one of the times I let loose without thinking, without stopping to think about what I was going to say, letting my feelings pour.

"You are wrong. She doesn't control me. She is one of the best things that has ever happened to me. She is nice, caring and...and sweet."

"Kevin. Wait a minute. What are you?..."

"She has her faults, of course, but I love her all the same. And being raised without a father doesn't mean anything!"

Then, I cut the call.

She was standing in front of me now, looking at the note. There was nowhere to run this time, and I had to face her. There was no rearview mirror to use to watch from a distance. There was no smile on her face either. Her eyes were filled with tears threatening to drop. It took a while before I realized my face mirrored hers, a sad reflection basking in her radiant glow. This was Megan, the woman I fell in love with, and her favorite strawberry donuts. I made to hug her, to reassure her that I was still there at least.

But she took one long look at me and walked out—the sound of a door being closed forcefully resonated throughout the house.

Chapter 17

Megan

♥

Day Fourteen: Tuesday

T he tune that streamed out of the iPod strangely reminded me of my wedding. It was a soft, lilting tune that sounded so ethereal that it gave me goosebumps. It was not played at my wedding or anything, but for some reason, it reminded me of it.

I sat at the kitchen counter, entranced by the ethnic vocalizing of the lady I could not see, yet grateful I could take part in enjoying the beautiful music she was sharing with the world. *Bliss. Just pure bliss.*

The donuts Kevin got me yesterday... with the strawberry filling. Another form of bliss.

I don't think I've ever had donuts that good since the ones he left me at work one Valentine's day some years ago. It was the second time I was ever serving him, and he did have a face that was hard to forget. I chuckled softly. That face was punched on my account the third time I saw him, though. *Memories...*

The note that accompanied it, though. It riled me up in many more ways than I had realized was possible. *Sorry?* Well, I was sorry too. Maybe it wasn't him I was angry at. Perhaps it was me and my many shortcomings.

It was only 6:18 in the morning, and I was already done with my laundry. I was up so early, even though I had no place to be exactly. I turned in my resignation to Leyton's mail last night. I had been planning on that for a while, but I guess Shlux helped fast-track the resignation plans. So, currently, I am in limbo. Or, you could say that I was semi-jobless.

I went to remove my clothes from the machine, and that was when I noticed that I had forgotten to put in my sweatshirt and running pants. I always check the pockets of my clothes before washing them since the way I washed up an important receipt with my jeans, ruined it, and I had to pay again.

There was a card in one of my pockets. *Could it be my missing credit card?* It had gone missing for about a month now. I pulled it out. It was the black business card the alley therapist guy gave me some mornings ago.

He did say I could come to him if I wanted to talk and like they say, there is no better time than the present. Just that, my present was also a tad messy– I was on the brink of a divorce, facing a career shift, and likely to move and move around a whole lot.

I thought about it for a bit, trying to weigh my options. *What is the worst thing that could happen if I go? What is the best thing that could happen if I go?*

At worst, it could be somewhere shady without air conditioning. At best, I'd have a swell time after letting my heart out to someone who would just listen with little to no judgment.

Shanice could, but she wasn't a certified therapist. Everything pointed to checking him out. Before going someplace, I'd have to look the establishment up online—better to be safe than sorry.

The place looked pretty decent online. *Third Floor. Stilton Building. Saddle Brook.* It wasn't too far away. I could stop there by noon and still have enough time to see Shanice.

I opted for a baby pink shift dress with layered ruffle sleeves. My trusty brown pumps and matching bag combo did not fail me this time.

I joined some three other people to get into the elevator. What was surprising was that we all wanted to get off on the third floor. Unless the floor had other enterprises, Eirene center had to be very busy.

I noticed some well-dressed people in the lobby, on their phones, some leafing through magazines. They seemed to be waiting for someone or something.

Occasionally, one person would get up and go into a room. It was all very organized, and I wondered why I had not heard of this place before. Needless to say, Eirene Center had quite the pick of clientele. One could tell that they were mostly people of the high class, yet they weren't exactly hoity-toity. It was as though the others weren't there and they were just keeping themselves company.

I had stood by the elevator for about two minutes, sticking out like a sore thumb, when the receptionist waved me over, a warm smile on her young face.

"How may I help you, ma'am? Do you have an appointment?"

I was immediately confused. He said I could come in anytime, but he didn't tell me anything about appointments.

"No, I'm afraid I don't. All I've got is this card," I said and handed over the black business card.

"Oh, Simmons. Come with me, please."

She led me to a metal door along the corridor with a nameplate that read: *A. J. Simmons.*

She knocked gently and opened the door with a crack. She muttered some things to the person inside and gestured for me to come in.

It was the man from that morning jog.

"Runner of the alleyway. Good day, ma'am. How're you doing?"

"Dark Knight. I'm doing just fine, you?" I turned to see that the lady had left us, and we were now alone. "Please, excuse me."

I turned the sound recorder on my phone and sent Shanice my location, just in case.

"What a nickname. Do have a seat, please," he said, pointing me to the rather soft, beige couch in front of a low center table. He left his swivel chair and came to sit in the armchair opposite me. The tasseled, velvet-covered throw pillows did add to the elegance of the expansive office.

The colors were muted, and the place was comfy; it made me feel so at ease. There was a tastefulness about the decor that wasn't stifling but made one feel...right at home.

"So, what brings you here today? It's been quite some days since our last interaction," he asked, a small smile playing on his rather sensuous lips.

"Yes, I've been caught up in work. Work I'd be leaving soon."

He clasped his hands in front of him. "Why, though? You're resigning?"

"Yes, I am. I'd be moving away after my divorce, which should be finalized this week, even though I don't know where I'd be going yet. I just know I'm leaving here. Anywhere but here...too many memories."

He nodded as though expecting me to continue. I must have talked too much again. Not me oversharing for no reason.

"I'm sorry, I was just rambling on...."

"No, none of that. You came here to talk, and talk, we shall. Plus, this might be the only time we get to meet, so let's maximize it, shall we?"

I nodded slowly, his soothing voice very nearly moving me to tears. His aura was so calming, and his stormy grey eyes made me feel like he could see through me and see my soul, so it felt needless to hide anything from him. I felt like he would understand. He would understand everything.

His calm voice was like a melody, slowly tuning out the cacophony that once besieged my mind.

"Why are you getting a divorce? I'm sure there was once a time when you loved your spouse...."

In a small voice, which I did not recognize as mine, I responded, "I still do."

"Then, what happened? They fell out of love?"

It was then I noticed two wet dots on my pink dress. Tears had slipped out without me even realizing it.

"I discovered he was cheating on me when I saw condoms in his pockets on the night of our seventh anniversary. Sure, I felt he had been a bit distant for a bit because of his work, so I even put in the effort to throw him a small party with few friends in attendance and all... I just didn't think the rift had grown so much...." My words trailed off as I felt a fresh round of tears pricking the back of my throat.

He sighed, his striking face the picture of sympathy.

"And I guess, for you, cheating is unforgivable?"

I shook my head. "Of course not. I was hurt and angry at first, but then I calmed down and was willing to talk things through. He then said he's been sick of our marriage for a long time and would like to get a divorce... apparently, he had met some lady at work, and she makes him happy."

"And how did you take the news? Any woman in your shoes will be angry..."

"It hurt. It...still hurts. I was there with him through thick and thin; even when his bitchy mother would not even come home to visit him when he had surgery, I was there. Working extra hours to earn enough to get him things he wanted, things I felt he deserved... he chose to throw all that away...." I found myself sobbing for a few minutes, and then I resumed talking after a bit.

"It's funny how he almost never remembers his own promises until I remind him. I decided that he would fulfill, at least, the main ones I can remember before I leave his life for good." I chuckled and continued, "Promises are made to be kept, after all."

He cocked his head to one side, studying me intently. "And how do you plan on achieving that, Runner?"

I laughed at that. I didn't even realize I had not yet told him my name and I had gone on yapping about my life's woes. What dolor can do to one...

"I'm sorry, I don't think I've introduced myself to you. I'm Megan Stewart...uh, Megan Beecroft soon."

He merely smiled at me. A smile I was sure must have turned many clients into crushes. "It's understandable. We both got carried away. You can continue, please."

"Well, since we didn't draft a prenup, I made him agree to a deal. To respond to my requests over a few days, which is to make him fulfill the promises he made all these years. I mean the ones he's yet to redeem."

"Hmmm, I see. Did he state any other reason apart from the other woman as his reason for wanting a split?"

"I guess he was just tired of me micromanaging him— where we went, who we hung out with, who I let into our circle— that sort of thing. I don't think I was doing that, though. I just wanted what was best for us, for our family."

Wisps of his wavy black hair fell into his face, and he pushed them back with his fingers. I swallowed. My mind was definitely not in a good place.

"Most people who micromanage others usually do so out of pure motives at first and don't know when it begins to stifle the other person. I wish he had communicated how he was feeling early enough instead of finding succor in another woman."

"But didn't you notice a change in his attitude towards you?"

I shook my head and bit down hard on my lip, trying and failing to hold back tears.

"You realize this does not make you a bad person, right? You were only protective of your family, but maybe a tad too protective. As it stands, we have to find a way to move forward."

"Yeah... I, uh, I got a job. That's why I'm moving away. I can't stay here anyway. Everything here reminds me of him, and I couldn't be more grateful this job came at this time. It's a much-needed distraction."

He nodded, and I could have almost sworn that he had been through something like this before. He looked like he could relate.

"It's not enough to distract yourself, Megan...."

Hearing him call my name in such a fatherly tone reminded me of the father I had but never met. He was young, no doubt about it, but he exuded confidence that spoke of wisdom far above his years.

"...you need to heal. You need to come to terms with the painful change and love yourself through it, regardless. This is not me promising that it would be all easy here on out or that there won't be nights where you'd cry yourself to sleep, but do not let it consume you. And while we're at it, beware of toxic positivity where you shove it so far down and also on a smiley face while trying to convince yourself and others that everything is okay."

We both sat in silence for a bit while I processed it.

"Do you understand what I mean?"

I nodded, feeling a lot lighter than when I first came into that office.

"I'm sure I can manage even that, at least."

The minute I stepped out of the office, I turned off the sound recorder, making a mental note to listen to the recording later.

A twenty-five minutes drive had me at Shanice's residence at Kearny. She had blown up my phone with texts asking about the therapist.

Tell me about questions like 'How's he like? Is he hot?'

Of course, questions like that had me in stitches. Yes, he was hot, but I sure as hell wasn't going to look at him that way. He's a man I would probably never see again, with the divorce coming up and this new job I'm taking on.

It would be wise for me to follow his advice– to let myself heal and love myself through all these shenanigans. *Oh, and I'd add one more for the road– I'd put myself first.*

I've had enough of my goodwill and love being taken for granted with Kevin. *Maybe while trying to be perfect for him, I have lost touch with who I really am, and I'd like to see this new phase as the path to self-discovery. I wonder what I have in store under all these wraps. Can't wait to find out!*

She handed me my glass of punch and plopped down on the sofa next to me, her eyes wide as saucers.

"You don't mean it. A travel photographer? As in traveling-round-the-world travel photographer?"

I laughed. "Yes. I was as surprised as you are, but I tried my best not to look interested."

"Hope you accepted, though?"

I took a big swig of my drink and stared into the distance. "Yeah, but it means I'd be moving around a lot."

She set her hand over mine and looked at me intently. "You've always been a free spirit, Megan. That you spent the last few years of your life in a stationary state never quite quelled that flame in you, and you know it. I frankly think you've denied yourself true happiness for so long. Get this one for you."

For me. For the first time in a long time, I knew what I wanted, and I sure was going for it.

Chapter 18

Kevin

♥

Day Fourteen: Tuesday

Kelly wanted us to meet. I wasn't particularly against the idea but I didn't really want to see her. Not at this moment. I was still in love with her, of course, but I needed space. I needed time to breathe, time to think. She was always at my office when I walked in, and these days, she had been texting me regularly too. The unspoken rule we had, is now in the dust. But it seemed important, and she wanted to meet for drinks. That meant an informal setting, probably a bar. But what did she want? Had she noticed my withdrawal the past few days and wanted to talk to me about it? Maybe that was why she chose somewhere that would be a change of scenery, away from the gym and our office.

There was no reason I wouldn't show. I didn't have much work at the office as she saw to it that I finished everything, helping where she could. So now that she asked for this, I didn't have any concrete excuse. I had to go.

I wore a black t-shirt and black trousers, and they adequately reflected my mood.

Bar Crusty. I'm waiting.

Come fast.

Kisses.

She sent me the message almost ten minutes ago, and I was already on my way. I took my car this time. It had been a long time since I was out at night. The roads were still busy, and I saw many people in casual wear, milling about with drinks in hand. It wasn't the weekend yet, but the atmosphere was in the air. I tucked my car in between a Range Rover and a convertible whose make I couldn't decipher.

There was something familiar about this particular bar. I felt like I had been here before. But I would have remembered a name like *Bar Crusty*. I entered the bar, and it all came flooding back. I had made a mistake. They must have undergone a change in management since I last came here with Megan. But whatever they had changed, the interior was the same. The brown stools facing the bar, with various bartenders attending to the numerous customers. It was a huge oval room, drawing inspiration from the President's office at the white house.

I stood at the door at the memories came rushing back. I wondered why Megan hadn't given me a note sending me here to get her favorite drink. Then again, I could guess why she wouldn't want to remember. We had come here during one of our spontaneous nights when we had felt bored and needed to unwind. We were both feeling wild and a walk around the block wouldn't do. It was called *The Bar Club.*

We wanted to dance the night away. I had gone to get drinks, and by the time I came back, I met Megan waiting by the door, asking to be taken back home.

"Why? What's the matter?"

"Just take me away from here, please."

The urgency in her voice couldn't be ignored. I led the way to the car, and we drove out immediately. She was in a bad mood for the next few days. I had learned early on that when she got like that, and it was better to leave her alone. She would tell me everything when she was ready. Though it took longer than usual for her to talk to me that time, she eventually spoke up, and I got angry. Not at her, at him. The Black Rider was at *The Bar Club.*

He had seen her and remembered who she was at once. He had called his friends, and together, they had barraged her with lewd comments while I was getting out drinks. I had even spent some time talking to the bartender about the Mets and their winning streak. I felt bile rise to my throat. The first time he was around, I was there to protect her from his onslaught, but now, in a club like that, she was left alone, versus him and his friends. They were gone before I came back. Thankfully, they hadn't touched her in any way. But I knew that Megan was prone to emotional assault more than any other despite her stoic demeanor most times in the face of such situations.

Now, looking at Kelly, there was no way she could have known that this place held such memories for me. And besides, I should be happy that I would be getting married to her soon. That was what we both wanted, and we would get it soon. I knew Megan wasn't going to cause any trouble with the divorce, provided I kept up my end of the bargain. So why wasn't I jumping for joy?

Kelly was wearing a short black gown. Outside the bar, we would have fit perfectly in a funeral procession but we blended in with others here.

"Kevin. Hey. You don't look so good."

I tried to smile, and immediately after I did that, she frowned. I should have known it was useless to fool her. She must have let a lot get past her these few days, but she wasn't stupid.

"Don't I?"

" Don't give me that. Don't you want to see me?"

I fell into a seat beside her.

"Is this seat taken?" I asked her knowing she was going to ignore me. She did.

"Kevin. What is it exactly?"

I didn't look at her. I turned to the bartender and asked for a dry Scotch. It was going to be a long night.

"Nothing is the matter, Kelly. I'm perfectly fine."

"You don't look fine. You came in here frowning like I did something wrong, only that's not possible because we just met now. So tell me what is going on, Kev."

Most times, the way she shortened my name reminded me of Megan, and it wasn't something I hated. But today, it seemed like she was trying hard to imitate her for some reason.

Calm down.

There was no reason for her to do that. I was starting to overthink again. The requests were coming to an end, and Megan would have to sign the papers the following morning, I thought. I had to keep things together until then. But Kelly wouldn't let it go.

"Kev? Are you there? You've zoned off again."

I heard her voice calling out to me, but it was from a distance. I was truly far gone. I had to come clean if we were to move forward.

"Okay, okay. I have something to tell you, Kel."

She settled down on her seat dramatically, but I could see the worry behind her eyes, the way her lashes hooded over them as if she was protecting herself from being hurt. But that was what I was about to do to her now.

"I have been lying to you for the past week, at least."

"Why? What happened exactly?"

I suddenly couldn't find the right words. How do you tell someone that you lied to them not to protect them but for no reason at all? How do you say you ignored several warnings and pleas and did the exact opposite of what they didn't want?

"I've been agreeing to Megan's requests. She never stopped sending them. I didn't tell you about it."

"I don't understand."

She looked really confused. Her hand kept dragging her hair back even when it wasn't entering her face.

"I've been agreeing to Megan's requests, Kel. But it's ending tomorrow, so...."

"What the hell, Kevin? What did you just tell me?"

Her voice was at a normal decibel, but it felt like she was screaming. I could see she was trying to control herself.

"Wait. It's not...."

"You've been going behind my back, doing whatever she tells you? Are you her dog?"

That statement hit home.

"Kelly, you have to calm down. I'm sorry I didn't tell you, but...."

She didn't let me finish.

"You're sorry. I asked you every day how the divorce proceedings were going, and you said they were going smoothly. Those were your words...."

"They *are* going smoothly. It's just till tomorrow and...."

"Oh my God!" she was shouting now. "You're still thinking of continuing till tomorrow? After everything, after lying? You're still thinking of tomorrow?"

I shouldn't have told her that. But it was better to come clean at once.

"No, wait. I mean, she'll sign the papers tomorrow, and we'll be free."

"Free? Were we shackled before? I specifically warned you not to do anything, that she was going to change you, but you didn't listen to me. Maybe she has gotten what she wanted already."

"Kelly. You are taking this too far."

"In taking it too far? You lied to me every day, nonstop. You looked me in the eye and lied to me. Without remorse or guilt... I warned you about this. That she was manipulating you with those requests."

"Kelly...It doesn't matter. She will sign the papers tomorrow, and that is it."

I didn't know what else to say. There was no excuse I could give.

"That was the lowest you could go, Kevin. You promised me you would never lie to me. You know how I hate lies, yet...."

Then, before I could say anything else, she picked up her bag and left. Leaving me in the wake of her cologne and the stares of those who had watched the encounter.

Chapter 19

Kevin

♥

Day Fifteen: Wednesday

Today is the last day for the requests, and everything will be over soon. I would finally be with Kelly, and we would live happily ever after and all that. I saw the note where she always left it. Once again, the events of the previous night reentered my mind. Was Kelly right? Was Megan trying to win me back in some way? She told me this was all for closure, that she needed to be free from everything and end our marriage knowing she tried her best. But was she manipulating me, too, killing two birds with one stone? Messing with my head so I would miss her so much that I would want her back when she eventually left?

There were more questions than answers, and I couldn't think of everything at once. It would be best to get it over with and move on with my life. I loved Kelly. Kelly loved me too. Nothing else mattered.

> *8. Remember how much you loved music? How we went to numerous concerts, and how you sing to me songs you composed for me?*

> *Doh that may be long forgotten now, could you write a song just for me, reminding me of the good times we shared?*

> *~Megan*

Yes, I once believed the music industry was where I was destined to be, but life taught me differently. It had been a long time since I composed anything. But as I read the note, I began to remember long-forgotten lyrics, mixing up with new lines my head was concocting. On my way to work, I had to pull my car over and over as I wrote the song on a piece of paper.

Unlike before, when I had to cancel outlines because they sounded cheesy, these flowed into each other seamlessly, and before long, I found myself singing along. I was enjoying what I was doing, and the memories we shared were flooding my thoughts. I couldn't think of anything else. I was happy, and after a very long time, I was truly happy.

I had to meet Kelly at the coffee shop we frequented on my way home. We didn't meet at work today. I was planning to apologize for last night and for the past few days. I parked in front of the shop and went in. Very few cars were parked outside, leading me to believe that the shop was almost empty. I was correct. Kelly was seated at the far end, and she picked the table farthest from the door. I knew this was because she would be able to watch my expression as I entered.

But I didn't care about that. I had composed a beautiful song, and it wouldn't leave my head. It was short and maybe even a bit cliché, but I knew Megan would love it. I didn't realize I was mouthing the lyrics until she called my attention to it.

"Kevin? What are you singing?"

She was smiling.

"I didn't know you sang, and you look so happy."

I *was* happy. But I had to apologize first.

"Hey, Kelly. Look, I'm sorry about everything. I don't know why I didn't tell you. I just want everything to be over. I'm so sorry."

"It's okay. I understand; I do. Don't do it again. We agreed the would be no secrets."

"From now on."

"You really look happy to see me. I was scared you would...I don't know."

She was blushing.

"Of course, I'm happy to see you. What else could I be happy about?

As I said that, I felt intense guilt. She thought I was happy to see her. Was I really? I was indifferent. What was on my mind then was Megan and her smile and how much she would like the song I had composed out of nowhere.

"I heard the song you were singing—*you and me into the horizon.* I didn't know you were that sweet, Kev. A song for me?"

She thought I was singing it for her. My guilt went as deep as I had ever felt. I felt like a cheat; I was a cheat. I cheated on Megan with Kelly, and now I felt like I was cheating on Kelly with Megan. Maybe I wasn't really cheating because I still wanted to be with Kelly, but... something was missing. I knew that now. Was that still cheating if you cheated on someone you cheated with? Even if it was with someone, you originally cheated on?

Was I cheating on Kelly with Megan? If I wasn't, then why was I feeling such guilt? All of a sudden, what I had to do became clear.

"You know what? There's going to be a festival near the waterfront tomorrow. Could we have our lunch there then?"

But at that moment, what was on my mind wasn't the festival or lunch with Kelly.

Chapter 20

Megan

♥

The Day

The strains of a classical music piece streamed out from my iPod next to me on the bed. I had used it as a paperweight for the divorce papers Kevin served me.

The tune was nostalgic, somewhat like it bore a memory just out of reach of my recollection. The more I tried to remember where I knew the melody from, the less I recalled it. It did not help that my little head was chuck-full of thoughts, none comforting. I closed my eyes, trying to still my mind.

Where did I miss it? It was hard to pinpoint that now. Kevin had co-operated with all my requests until now—the gifts, the food, the flowers, the movie outing. He even stood up to his mum because I asked him to, and I realize that could not have been easy on him.

The tears that pushed against my eyelids found sites of escape at my eye corners, running till they pooled in my ears.

He had been, at the bare minimum, civil and considerate. He saw no reason to have his girlfriend over since I still live here. It may not seem like much but I'm not sure I can say for sure what my reaction would be if he did that. It's his apartment too, and his guests are none of my business, so I'm grateful he didn't.

Something tells me, though, that it was not for my sake, but circumstances just haven't called for it yet.

With Kevin, one could never tell. All the more reason I have to leave this place as soon as possible.

Like with the gifts, it was hard to place whether he did them out of the goodness of his heart, out of guilt of unfulfilled promises, or he just wanted me out of his hair as quickly as he could.

From all that he said on the night of our seventh anniversary, he had been unhappy for a long time, so little wonder he's doing everything I ask so he can move this up quickly. He was indeed very clear when he iterated that these sweet little errands would not stir up any old emotions in him. I get it. I really do, but I'd have felt cheated if he couldn't redeem, at least, the most basic of the promises he made. He made them of his own volition, after all, so he was obligated to follow through with them.

I sat up and resolved to begin packing my stuff. I booked an early evening flight so at least I could see the sunset, and I even paid extra for a window seat. I had just one job now, and I sure as hell was going to do it to the best of my ability. Moreover, it was something I already enjoyed, so why not fully enjoy it as I should?

My suitcases were still in my closet, and while I had quite a few of them, I doubted all my clothes would fit in these bags. Also, nomads don't need much. Chances are that I'd be buying clothes suitable for the various climates I fly to, so I only need a few clothes, anyway. I could have Kevin help donate the clothes or something... no, that would be too much of a hassle. I could haul them over to Shanice's instead. She'd be more than happy to give them away.

Many of my personal effects were still in the room we once shared. I wasn't sure I could stomach seeing that place. For me, it was not just a room. It was a sanctuary, a sacred spot of sorts. A sacred spot I was no longer allowed to worship in.

I stared longingly at my small– well, not-so-small– closet and wondered if I would truly have the heart to genuinely separate what I should take along from pieces I was only nostalgic about, like that chunky white knit pullover that stared at me from where it was hung.

Basics. I'd stick to only basics. *Plain tees in white, black, grey, and beige. Hiking shorts. Wide-leg pants. Black slacks. A denim jacket. A maxi sundress. Sneakers and a pair of ankle boots for running around.* That was pretty much about it.

I was very tempted to put pictures of Kevin and me in my carry-on bag. I had them in my grasp already, but I paused. The point of this divorce and moving away was to let go of the shackles of the past and not to further ensnare me by holding on to relics that have now lost meaning.

With that, I tossed the envelope back into the box, but only after selecting pictures that had just me and the girls in them– and those were not many. It would be nice to look at the friends that helped me in my darkest days while I'm in a different time zone and can't be interrupting their daily lives or sleep. I'd definitely try to reach out, though. Keeping in touch is the least I can do.

And that habit will have to be cultivated right from the get-go. I glanced at the time on my phone—*10:38 am.*

Andrea should be on a break right about now; Candace is a full-time housewife, and Shanice works from home. No better time than now if I wanted to catch these women. A conference call would do.

Candace connected immediately, then Andrea. Tori also joined in almost immediately, toothbrush in mouth.

"Hello there!" came Andrea's cheery voice, evoking a sincere smile from me.

"Hey…" I tried my best to sound as animated as possible, but Tori clearly wasn't having it.

She spat out the toothpaste foam so she could throw a jab in my direction. "Look alive, nomad! I know you can't wait to traipse the world in your little adventurer boots, but at least look excited to see us, aye?"

There was a way she phrased her words that made it just impossible not to like her. She had such a large heart, and that did not dwindle her penchant for sarcasm one bit.

Candace chipped in, always quick to defend me. "Now, now, Tori... at least she tried to smile! You give us a smile of your own...."

I gave a small laugh, wondering when these two would ever stop bickering. It was taking quite a bit of time for Shanice to join in, and I was starting to worry I had called at the wrong time.

"Hallo!" she drawled as her pretty face popped up in a square on the screen. "I'm sorry, I just had to finish up the editing of a video. It's scheduled to go up tonight. You all better watch it...regardless of where in the world you may be. And yes, Megan, it's you I'm referring to."

Trust Shanice to come up with all this... she was drama personified. Andrea looked a little lost.

"Uh, guys... I don't get it. Why is Megan traveling? I mean, where's she going?"

Candace tutted, shaking her head as one would at an impertinent child. "Duh... her new job?" Andrea blinked, still not getting it, so Candace continued. "As a travel photographer? Do you not read the group chat's messages?"

"Oh..." A guilty look crossed Andrea's face. "Well, I haven't been following. Work has had me in a pinch of late."

"Make you should try something more liberating...." Shanice suggested and was soon backed up by Tori.

"Maybe something as freeing as travel photography. How I envy you, girl! Vacation every six months, twice a year!"

We all shared great laughs after that. It felt so refreshing to be able to converse with them, yet sad that it would be a while before I'd be able to see them physically again. Right as we were about to end the call, I remembered the clothes I wanted to donate to Shanice's green earth and body positivity cause of recycling, thrifting, and recycling clothes. She'd find people to give. Most likely, people who need it. Whatever she did with them was not my business, per se. I just wanted the clothes gone.

"Yeah, so Shanice, I have a couple of clothes and shoes I want to donate, seeing that I may not be back in NJ anytime soon."

"Wow! Great. Send them right over. It would be of great help to many. I'm glad you thought of donating them..."

"There we go...Megan's activated the darn Mother Theresa."

"Oh, shut up...."

As soon as the call dropped, I called a moving company who said they'd be here in ten. They got here in under fifteen minutes, so I guess that's fast enough. They were a bit underwhelmed though when they saw that all I required them to move were two boxes and a large suitcase.

I went with them, with my camera in tow. It would be nice to catch a glimpse of the city, both with my eyes and lenses, before I bode the bustling city farewell.

I rode in front, beside the driver, observing the gloomy sky. Grey clouds punctuated the blue skies, blurring the sun's intense effect. The droplets from the van's very recent visit to the carwash sat on the windows, giving it a mottled, glossy finish.

I took a picture of the buildings, perfectly capturing the bustle of the city right before those towering walls. I saw a newlywed couple and their well-wishers stream out of an Orthodox Church. Their joy was so contagious that I could not help but take a picture of the scene. I was happy for them, but there was no mistake about it– there was a lurch in my chest on seeing that harmless happy scene. So yes, I was going to keep the picture to remind myself that true love and happiness exist out there, and every day, I inch closer and closer to it. It may hurt right now, but one day, I'd be able to look at this joyful day of this unknown, faceless couple and not feel any pain whatsoever.

The pictures had water drop effects on them due to the wet windows I was photographing through, but I couldn't care less. They made the pictures prettier anyway, adding a somewhat vintage touch to them.

Within thirty minutes, we had gotten to Shanice's residence in Kearny. She bounded out of her home, her excitement reminding me of a little puppy. Her energy was infectious, I must admit.

She gave me a full hug, nearly crushing my ribs as she squeezed me tight and tilted me from side to side.

"Argh, baby girl! I'd miss you for sure! I wish I were still staying next door...maybe the goodbyes wouldn't be so bad."

I could see the glassy beads that were forming in her eyes. If the burning at the back of my throat was any indication, my eyes certainly did mirror hers on hearing that sentence.

She invited me in for some coffee, and while the offer was rather tempting, I had to decline as I wasn't sure I was entirely done packing, and I wanted to be at the airport before the time of my flight.

"Or you could leave for the airport from here while we catch up. Your stuff is with you?"

I shook my head and said, "Nah. They're back home. I'd have to go pick them up." I stopped talking immediately and clasped my hand over my mouth, willing myself not to cry. Shanice engulfed me in a bear hug and held me till I stopped crying.

I got back to my apartment some twenty-five minutes later and met the iPod still playing music, mindlessly perched on the divorce papers.

I picked up the pen from the bedside drawer and glanced through the document. *Is this real? Is this Kevin finally telling me he's done?*

Maybe I should stop thinking that way and start to view it as an opportunity to discover myself and forge new ties with new people.

He would have kissed back the other night if he still was attracted to me. His refusal spoke volumes in itself. If it was just a rough patch, I'm sure his reaction would have been different. But it's a split for good.

With that, I signed my name at the bottom of the last page, sighing as I felt a huge burden slip off my shoulders.

Instinctively, I massaged my left ring finger, rubbing soft flesh where a hard ring once stood. I placed the document on the center table, unsure whether or not to leave a note. I decided to leave a note for closure.

I fished out the last of the pink index cards I had originally bought for our anniversary treasure hunt and scribbled a hasty note.

> *Thank you for all the gifts. Now here's one for you.*

> *~ Megan*

Next to the note, I dropped the signed divorce papers and keys to the house.

As I walked out the door with my carry-on bag in hand, I suddenly remembered the tune.

It was the tune of the first waltz Kevin, and I danced as a couple. It was so long ago it felt like it was an experience from a past life or a dream from yesteryears.

Chapter 21

Kevin

The Day

I thought it would be harder to find the lyrics and what tune would align with them. I assumed it was supposed to be a love song, but then I couldn't be too sure. She could want an ordinary song about life and its struggles. But I didn't care anymore. I had come to realize that despite our differences and faults, I had greatly enjoyed the time we spent together.

The chords flowed, and the music was intense. I could feel emotions stirring within me as I wrote it. I didn't need a guitar to fill in the chords, and I didn't need to sing it out and see if it was good. I knew I had created something intense.

"Hey, are you going to the festival?"

One of my colleagues had barged into my office. Tim Anderson. He was a divorcee who had left his previous wife, whom he claimed to love so much, and went to meet someone else we didn't know about. He had invited us over to dinner many times. Megan and I. His wife was charming, and it was hard to imagine there were any irreconcilable differences.

He had been married for over a year now, and I hadn't gotten any invitations. I didn't know who his wife was, and there was some sort of chasm between us. We were once close and went home on the subway together.

Was that how we were going to be? If we divorced, would I start separating myself from my friends, albeit unknowingly? What about Megan and me? Would we still be friends? Would she remarry?

Suddenly the thought of Megan with another man made me sick. The thought of another man putting his hands around her made me frown so deeply that Tim noticed.

"Kevin. Are you with me? Earth to Kevin. Are you there?"

He snapped his fingers in front of my face before I was able to recover.

"Sorry, Tim. I was just thinking about something for the next contract. What's up? It's been a long time. How's Sloan?"

"Susan. Her name is Susan, Kevin. Is there something up with you, man?"

"No. Why would you think so?" I queried.

"You always make the mistake of calling her Sloan. And every time, I correct you. At a point, I thought you were doing it on purpose."

He looked at me with a wry smile.

Okay, maybe I had been doing it on purpose. It was a way of me trying to tell him that I didn't know his wife and that he had not properly introduced us. He didn't do a grand wedding, but I still wasn't invited. He had claimed it was an oversight. That they only invited close family members of both the bride and groom. But I was hurt nonetheless.

"Why would I do that? Come on. I'm a bit distracted. That's all," I replied to his accusations.

"You haven't answered me. How's Megan? I haven't been getting her usual checkup calls these past few weeks. Is she angry with me?"

I had no idea of the calls, but I wasn't surprised. It was something Megan would do.

"No, she isn't angry with you, Tim. I guess her work has been a bit hectic these days."

Tim nodded.

"That's okay. You guys are okay, aren't you? I have been seeing you around with Kelly...."

He didn't complete his sentence, and I didn't say anything about it either. We sat down for a few seconds staring at each other, not saying anything, and I wasn't offering him any explanation.

"Rumors have been flying around the office about you two. There *is* nothing, yes?"

I shook my head, not in denial but in exasperation. Tim always wanted to know everything going on while keeping his own personal affairs out of listening range.

"Come on, Tim. Why not say what you were here for?"

He laughed.

"Wanted to ask if you were going to the festival at the waterfront? It looks like everyone is going there."

Kelly had asked us to eat lunch there, and I had completely forgotten. I had to call her, but I didn't want to leave the song I was writing.

"I might check it out," I didn't want to go with him, "But there's something I want to do here."

"Oh, yeah. Sure. I'll be along then. See you there."

Immediately after he left, I checked my phone. There were six missed calls from Kelly. She had been trying to get ahold of me for a while now. I hurriedly finished up and went to meet her. My song was finished.

"You're late."

Kelly had to shout for me to hear her over the din. The crowd was in a frenzy. Apparently, some guest artists had been sighted already, and one was already on the stage. The crowd was massive.

The festival was put together by an organization that I had never heard about. Apparently, they got the idea that artists, when asked to perform a show for charity, would rarely refuse. So they had called some top-performing musicians from across the country, and here they were. Though some had given some excuses- preparation for tours and illnesses, the majority had promised they would show up.

So, the anticipation was intense. There were a few naysayers who didn't believe any A-list artiste would turn up but here they were, and the crowd was increasing by the minute.

"I'm sorry. I got caught up in work and completely forgot. Really sorry, babe."

I said as I kissed her on her cheek. That seemed to do the trick as her face brightened up, and that smile that always enraptured me.

"What's with the guitar?"

I hadn't noticed that I carried it along. It was in my car as I was practicing and on my way here. I had taken it in hopes that...I didn't really know. I had heard that the festival was a charity event and I thought I could perform. It was a thought that occurred to me in the heat of my songwriting, but I didn't think I would follow through. But here I was with the guitar.

"…Guitar? Kevin?"

I had zoned out again.

"I need to speak to the organizers of this fest. Do you know anyone?"

Kelly's smile returned to her face.

"Don from Marketing is working with them, I think. He owes me a favor. What exactly are you planning?"

I didn't give her an answer to the question she asked.

"Could I speak to him?"

"Yeah. I know where he is."

That was it about Kelly. She was proactive and always wanted to help in any way she could. She took me around the crowd to the back of the staging area. The guards let her around. It was then I noticed she had a VIP pass.

"How did you get that?"

She was walking past barriers set up. They stepped aside for us once they looked at the tag around her neck.

"My parents are part of the sponsors. So, mum sent me a pass in case I decided to come."

It was all about giving back to people living with cancer, with the proceeds made from ticket sales going to those who have been diagnosed with the incurable disease. It was a noble cause, and I appreciated the idea, but that wasn't what I was thinking about at the moment.

"Hey, Don. I need a favor from you."

She said without any form of the preamble. She was in boss mode. I had seen this a couple of times when she was speaking to subordinates.

"Hey. What's up? I didn't think you were going To show up."

Don looked like a bouncer with his huge biceps and his stoic demeanor. It was hard to imagine someone like that behind a desk.

"Yeah. I changed my mind. My friend here wants something."

The man she called Don looked doubtful, but Kelly's gaze didn't leave his face. I observed the exchange between them for a while. It was tense, but she didn't back down. She didn't even know what I wanted, although she could have guessed from the guitar I was holding. What did I want? Would Megan understand what all this meant? Was I doing it for her? Why was I doing it in the first place?

From the look on Kelly's face, she probably thought I wanted to sing for her. I was so confused. In a way, I wanted Don to refuse. I would just write Megan the song or record it while singing in my car.

I could hear the shouts of the crowd. They were increasing by the minute. I wanted to back out.

"What do you want?"

He was talking to me, and his voice was harsh, but Kelly was looking at me in expectation.

"I would like to perform." His eyes went wide. "I know, I don't mean during the main time, like a break or in-between performances. Five minutes is all I need, really. It's for someone I love very much."

I could see Kelly blushing. Her eyes fluttered, and I could have sworn there were tears. The guilt I felt, the guilt that had receded to the background, now came running up front, squeezing my heart and making me uncomfortable. She thought I was singing it for her.

Don looked at both of us and sighed. He must have read or *misread* the situation.

"Well, you're on in ten minutes. I'll have to make some changes, but we're good." Turning to Kelly, he said, "I guess this means we're good." Then, he walked off, talking into his walkie-talkie, leaving us there.

"You didn't warn men beforehand. I could have helped you prepare."

I smiled for the first time since I first saw her here. She was sweet and didn't deserve what I was doing to her. This was cheating on some level. It had to be. I didn't trust myself to speak.

We saw Don raise three fingers and point to his watch.

"Okay. I'm going back to stay among the audience. I'll be right there cheering for you, Kev."

She didn't know if I could sing but was offering her support already. I wasn't one for stage fright, but I saw the number of people waiting to see their favorite superstars, and I would appear in front of them.

They were bound to boo me off the stage. They mainly were employees who decided to come here to unwind after a hard day's work. The event would also be streaming live on YouTube. I didn't know if Meagan had heard about it, but knowing her, she probably would have and was probably watching at the moment.

I texted her the YouTube link anyway.

The Song I wrote for you,
Streaming live at 12.15 pm.
~Kevin

I walked up the stage as my name was called. Taking the mic from Don, I turned to face the crowd, and I was daunted. I had never seen such a gathering in my life. I tuned them out of my head and sat down on the seat. I could feel my hands shaking. Maybe this was stage fright, but I didn't care anymore. I was too far gone to go back.

I was ready, but my tongue wouldn't move. And for some reason, I could remember the lyrics perfectly, but the tune had flown out of my head. I could hear the boos already. I thought of Megan and if she was watching this.

No matter how much she hated me, she would not want
me to mess this up.

Intro:

> *Rolling in the hay with*
> *someone else,*

> *Turning with every dip*
> *and crest,*

> *But you were there*
> *watching, tears in your*
> *eyes.*

I strummed the guitar for the interlude and noticed the
crowd had stopped booing. I was blank initially when I
started, pushing away the emotions threatening to run me
over, trying not to let the jeers get to me. But now, I could
keep them at bay any longer.

The jeers had stopped, and I could feel my emotions
sweeping over me. Kelly looked confused. My lyrics. She
knows I was singing *about* her, not *for* her. There was no
going back now.

Verse:

Heartbeats,
constrictions in your
chest.

I never thought I'd feel
this way.

You   waited,   you
pushed,   and   you
smiled, my little muse.

The memories we had,
the fights, the laughs.

I cherish them, my
muse, and I hope this
song reaches you.

They were enraptured now. I could feel their attention washing over me, folding me in and surrounding my being.

This was how it felt, singing before an audience that didn't want you to stop. And then I began the chorus.

Chorus:

I'm in love. I'm in love.

I never left for my heartbeats on.

I'm in love, oh my love.

My little flower, what have I done?

You gave me your all, the best and the worst.

And I threw it all away, and now It burdens like a cross.

Verse:

I remember the gifts,
your beliefs, and all
your dreams.

They are a part of
me, alongside my very
being.

I know I've lost it all.

Your undying love, our
future, and more.

But I still cherish them,
my muse, and this song
is for you.

Chorus:

I'm in love. I'm in love.

I never left for my heartbeats on.

I'm in love, oh my love.

My little flower, what have I done?

You gave me your all, the best and the worst.

And I threw it all away, and now it burdens like a cross.

The applause was deafening. They were screaming and shouting at the top of their voices. I had the courage to take a bow. But as I looked among the teeming crowd, I couldn't find Kelly anymore.

Chapter 22

Megan

The Day

When I hailed a taxi to head back to Shanice's to see her for the last time, I didn't think I would feel this... light and airy. I had been feeling terrible these past weeks; for once, I was starting to see how this could be a good thing. I was just close-minded to it then.

I could also vividly see the auburn and orange hues that were starting to sweep through New Jersey, casting a whimsical filter over the usual landscape.

I tried my best to soak up the sights and sounds of the city, the thrums, honks, and babble sounding to me like the performance of an exotic symphony. One I hoped to hold dear to my heart. There was no saying when next I'd be back in this city I had grown so accustomed to.

I was peering out the window when I felt my purse vibrate. My phone buzzed with a message. It was a link to some stream. I debated clicking on it, but I did it anyway.

It was the live video of a sing-off with a lot of people in attendance. *Hmm, looks interesting...*

The shock I got from seeing who was on stage was so massive I just sat still, transfixed. Unmoving. Unblinking.

Kevin was there on stage with his guitar slung across his body. His voice was still as silky as ever. His visualization game was on point, and the way his eyes roved the audience, as though trying to connect with them, was so magical.

What stood out to me the most, though, was how deep the lyrics ran. It was the most vulnerable confession I've heard him utter in public since our wedding vows, and there was a fat chance that he wasn't referring to just me in the song.

I did ask him to write me a song...no doubts there. I just did not think he'd perform it in public. I was expecting a voice note or a phone recording at best, only to be stunned by a public performance with hundreds, if not thousands, of people in attendance, both online and on-site.

It brought tears to my eyes, the thoughtfulness, the scale of planning, and the grit it would have required to pull this off. I watched him sing his heart out, and his emotions were conveyed in every flexion of his muscles. I was convinced he meant what he was singing. He appeared to be very particular about his wording in the lyrics. Even if it was a generic love song to everyone else, to me, it was our story he was painting.

Intense lyrics enmeshed in wonderful melody, delivered in his characteristic euphonic voice– mesmerizing enough to have anyone in a choke hold, but not me, not anymore.

The tears that now escaped my eyes were not those of longing or regret but exhaustion, slight anger, and faint amusement even.

We were too far gone for this. For us, it was too late. *To be honest, that last sentence is no longer valid, as there is no longer an 'us.'* It was, frankly, just too late for Kevin to make any retribution that could have any effect. I had given him more than enough time to fix up and make amends. He did not utilize all of those, but now, he's trying to patch things up through a soppy lovesick puppy song. That won't cut it. Not this time. Not anymore.

There was a spring in my step as I descended in front of the grey and teal semi-detached duplex where Shanice lived with her family. I was now light and free and deserved to walk as such. Light. Free. Airy. Unrestrained. Free to roam the length and width of the world. Free to take pictures of exotic sunsets. Free to live. Free to be.

I twirled in place, filling my lungs with the crisp autumn air. I spun around to see Shanice standing at her doorstep, staring at the level of weird behavior I was displaying at the entrance of her heavenly abode.

"What the heck? What got you excited? Have you somehow managed to win the lottery?"

I laughed, edging her to get into the house. "No, nothing that grand, I'm afraid. I just signed the divorce papers, and I suddenly realized how free I have now become."

Shanice sighed and moved to the kitchen. She brought out two glasses and a pack of chilled orange juice. As she filled the glasses, she iterated, "You've always been free. I think it's just a bit sad that you only realized that after getting a divorce."

We were both quiet for some seconds after that. Then she spoke up again.

"You cried on your way here, didn't you?"

I wanted to shake my bead in the negative, but then she pointed her warning index finger at me. "I can see the tear streaks, you know?"

I burst out laughing for some odd reason. There was nothing in the tiniest bit funny about what she just said, but the laughter came out of its own accord. I quickly brought it under control.

"Yeah, I did. But that was only because Kevin sent me a touching song. Not like I was down in the dumps or anything. Here, let me show you."

Shanice looked at me disbelievingly as if wondering where I would whip out a video of Kevin singing me a song. Her expression was like she was strongly suspecting me of having gone batshit crazy. And I couldn't blame her. Kevin singing me a song is one of the wildest things one could imagine. I honestly can not remember the last time he did that, even more surprising, right before a large crowd. He didn't call out my name or anything, but still...

I brought out my phone and opened the message that had the link. Shanice looked at me weirdly and inched closer, very interested in what I had to show her.

She sat, enthralled by his four minutes, twenty-eight-second performance. Now, please don't ask me why I have the figures stuck in my head. I may or may not have watched it a couple of times on my way to Shanice's.

"Girl... this... this is good! What're you gonna do now?"

I rolled my eyes. "What do you mean by what am I going to do?" *This chick gotta be seriously joking if she thinks I'd go running back to him because of some silly love song. That can never be me.*

She pulled my legs and teased me for quite a bit. I was enjoying the conversation so much that I nearly forgot my flight was by 8 pm, meaning I had to set out by five and be there within thirty to thirty-five minutes. An extreme sport, but still doable.

"Megan, it's 4:53. Your flight!"

"Oh my... I have to go now then... send my love to the gang and my babies."

I snatched my bag from the couch and was almost at the door when she called out, "Let me drive you!"

She dashed upstairs to get her car keys. It turned out they were on the kitchen counter. We threw the doors open at 4:57 to see Kevin at the door, his hand poised like he was about to knock. He looked stupefied yet relieved to see me.

"Oh, wow. Hello, Shanice. Megan...I need to talk to you... just this one last time."

"Well, this is me trying not to miss my flight. In almost behind schedule."

He pointed to the car he parked on the street. "I can drive you there, then. All I just want to do is get a chance to talk to...."

I cut him off before he had a chance to finish his pitiable sentence.

"Shanice already offered. It'd be rude to change plans suddenly because you came along."

He looked past me at Shanice pleadingly. She just leaned against the lintel and sold me out.

"It's alright. Let Kevin drive you. I'm supposed to put the roast in the oven by bow for tonight. Dinner has to be ready early... it's a school night!"

I shot her my most iconic I-will-get-you-back-for-this look, she responded to that with a push of her jaw and went back into the house.

"Alright then. Thank you, but let's speed up. Newark Airport."

"Sure, got it."

The silence in the car was deafening. Not even the radio was on. He came all the way, claiming he had something to say, and now he was quiet? Maybe he had thought better of it and realized it was a pointless, lame move. I could see the white and yellow lights of the airport slowly coming into view.

It was supposed to be an 18-minute drive, and for about fifteen minutes, all Kevin was doing was curling and uncurling his fingers around the steering wheel.

"Um, Megan. We need to talk."

"Yes, you said so earlier," I retorted, cutting him off sharply. If he had anything today, he had better go ahead with it because time was not a luxury I could afford, and neither did I want to listen to him, truth be told.

"I'm sorry. I know I'm flawed and severely lacking... I... mistreated you even though you were only good to me. I'm so sorry I cheated on you."

He burst into tears, startling me. I was stunned, hearing all that he was saying.

"You didn't deserve all that bullshit I was serving you. I'm really, really sorry, Megan. I don't know if you'd ever find it in your heart to forgive me."

I just stared at him, unseeing, confused at the words I was hearing him emit. He did look rather sad, sniffling and speaking, so I couldn't help but feel sorry for him.

Now? Now, he wanted to make up? Now he was sorry?

"I don't think I can ever find what I found in you in anyone else. I don't know what pushed me to make all those poor choices, but darling...."

"Megan. Call me Megan."

I saw the pained look that crossed his features, but I couldn't care less. All that did not matter to me anymore. We've split, and that's that.

"Megan... I know you're still angry, but I can't imagine spending the rest of my life without you being it. Please, another chance... please."

At this point, he was practically bawling. It made me feel somewhat bad.

"Kevin. Let's park for a bit."

We pulled over to a side of the road, knowing we could not stay there for long, but we needed that break. If not, we risked having an accident, which by any standard was a lot worse.

He looked at me, tears unabashedly running down his now flushed face. "I was wrong. I was wrong about you, about what I wanted, about my choice of actions... I was wrong, Megan, I admit. But please, let me fix this. I can't risk losing you. I need you; I can't go through life without you by my side, Megan. We've come a long way... We... We can fix this...."

Listening to his lachrymose monologue was starting to unsettle me, and I really did not want to snap at a man who was just trying to offer a maybe-sincere apology for his past misdemeanors.

"Kevin. Kevin, listen to me. It will not work. It did not work then, so why do you think it will now? It's always about you, you, you! Did you stop to consider how I was feeling in the marriage and how I'm feeling now? I was never your priority. Today, you feel like this, but I'm sure after a few days, you'd go back to being your regular self."

He bowed his head and sighed deeply. It was discomfiting seeing him look so vulnerable, but I knew what I wanted, and I stood my ground. And I was proud of myself for it.

The heavy silence that hung within the confines of the car kept us pondering for a few minutes. I suspect I was rather harsh in my speech, so I spoke again in softer tones, this time.

"Don't beat yourself up, though. Even the best of us make mistakes. Many have, and many will. You got distracted, and you made a hasty decision. Who hasn't? But we all have to live with the consequences of our decisions either way."

I watched him sit there in silence and glanced at my phone. *5:20 pm.* I really did not have any time to waste if

I did not want to miss my flight. I debated telling him or reminding him so as not to come across as insensitive, but this was work-related, and I sure as hell was not going to use my money to pay for a flight all because I missed the one the company paid for.

"Um, Kevin... my flight is in a few minutes."

He rubbed his face, cleaning his tears. "Yeah, that's true. My bad."

He got down and came to open my door. I don't remember the last time he ever did that or even the last time we rode together. As he handed me my luggage, he held my wrist, forcing me to stay on the spot.

"Please, don't go. Please."

I looked at him, somewhat sad at how dejected he looked. He reminded me of a stray puppy left in the rain. His eyes pleading, nearly doubled in despair. There was no denying that he was distraught, or at least giving a decent performance of it. I don't know why part of me still strongly felt like he was putting up a show. That part of me greatly doubted his true motives. *How can a person who claims to love me vacillate so quickly at the behest of another woman?*

But there was a hint of sincerity in those bright, glassy eyes.

Without thinking, I enveloped him in a hug, inhaling his pine and sandalwood scent for what would be the last time.

"Let's be best friends, Kevin. I'd send you postcards from around the world– or whatever keepsakes people send each other these days," I said and gave a nervous chuckle.

He didn't respond, and I could feel moisture along my shoulder and towards my back. I knew it was not precipitation, at least not the kind that fell from the skies, but the type that stemmed from regrets of yesteryears.

He held on to me, refusing to let go until some cars behind Kevin's car that wanted to get ahead started honking. At first, Kevin ignored them. I had to tap him.

"Looks like you have to move the car... And I have to go."

He pulled away grudgingly, his arms brushing mine as he pulled away. His fingers grazed the skin of my wrist, and where there once used to be a romantic tingle, now sat a dead sea of indifference, tending slightly towards aversion.

I felt sorry for him as I mouthed my last word to him.

"Bye."

Chapter 23

Kevin

The Day

They never stopped clapping. The applause was overwhelming. I could still hear the whistles and the shouts of *Bravo* renting the air. I loved it and basked in the euphoria as it washed over me. Then, Don, who was indeed in charge of the show, came up to me on stage as I was about to leave.

"That was a nice song, Kevin." Turning to the crowd, he shouted, "Come on y'all. Give it up for Kev!"

I had never heard such a loud sound in all my life. It was completely wonderful.

"Could you tell us who the song is about? Who did you write the song for?"

I looked at the crowd and saw Kelly waving at me. The cheers had died down a bit as everybody wanted to listen to what I had to say. Suddenly, I couldn't take it anymore.

I thought the lyrics would have made it clear to Kelly what I felt, but it seemed she hadn't paid much attention to it. The dam holding back my emotions broke as I let it all out.

"I wrote this song for the love of my life. I wanted to let her know how I felt about her. How much I love her."

I could feel the tears pushing against my eyes, threatening to fall. But I held it back. I wasn't going to see tears. Not in front of all these people.

"Wow. Whoever your love is, she is one lucky girl. Let's give it up for Kev once again."

"I don't know about that. But I'm lucky to have her. And after today, I don't know if I should call her my ex, my wife, or my best friend."

There was a moment of silence where they all tried to process what I had just said. Then, someone started clapping. Then another and another, and before long, they were all clapping, nodding, and singing the chorus of the songs I had just sung.

This time, I didn't wait to acknowledge the applause. I was beset with clarity of mind at that moment. I knew what I had to do, what I should have done a long time ago. I looked right at the camera. The tears in my eyes couldn't be hidden anymore.

"Megan, I don't know if you're watching, but I love you so much. I do, and I'm so sorry for everything."

I ran down the stage, but Kelly was in my way already.

"Think about what you're doing. What about us? What would happen to us now?"

I didn't know the answer to give her. There was nothing I would say that would soothe the pain she was feeling. In a way, we looked the same, trying to hold on to someone we know is lost to us already. The main difference being I caused everything that had happened to me myself. There was nobody else to blame. Not Kelly or Megan. Just good ol' me.

"I'm sorry, Kelly. Please let me go. I'm sorry I hurt you, but I still love her."

There was nothing else to say. In one minute, we had said it all, but she wasn't letting go easily.

"She manipulated you," she spat. "I warned you not to accede to her requests, but you didn't listen, and now you're running back to her. This isn't fair, Kevin. I gave you everything."

She was rambling. I was grateful there weren't any cameras here. This was one part of my confession I didn't want on YouTube. She was crying openly now. Her mascara was starting to run, and the whites of her eyes were more red than white.

"She manipulated you, and you're to go running with your cap in hand, begging her to take you back? What would happen to me now, Kevin? Don't you care anymore?"

I glanced at my watch. Megan was home now. I didn't want to call her. I wanted to tell her how sorry I was face to face.

"I've got to go, Kelly."

I turned my back and hurried to my car, ignoring the guilt I felt, the heart-wrenching feeling threatening to rend my heart in two. Maybe I didn't deserve any of them, but I could try to ask Megan for forgiveness. My heart, that same heart that was full of guilt, was also filled with love. I still loved Megan, and I was ready to do anything to get her back. But first, I had to get her to forgive me.

I was too late. The house was empty. Megan was gone. She had packed her bags and left the house empty and devoid of emotion and color. I had run into the house, and it had hit me with its vacuum-like sound. At once, I had known that the love of my life was gone.

I had stepped into her room to confirm. All her clothes were gone. I sat on the edge of the bed we once shared, and it looked spotless. The cream sheets blended with my shirt, the way my feelings were mixed and mashed together. I didn't know what to do. I realized I could call her, but I didn't know what to say. How do you deliver an apology of that magnitude over the phone? I also wondered if she had listened to the song I made for her and if she had watched me sing her a serenade in front of thousands of people.

I went to the fridge, where she put all the notes she had written. I was devastated. My heart was crying out in its pain, morning for what I had surely lost. I took all the notes and placed them on the kitchen counter. I could still smell the lavender scent that made me heady each time. *Her* lavender. But something else jumped at me.

Some of the notes contained words that were emboldened. I wondered why I hadn't noticed them before. It was just like Megan hiding a message within a message. My heartbeat went a notch higher as I spread the notes out, arranging them chronologically. Then, I saw it. And I cried more.

*1. Remember the gift I got you at that gift shop? That was the first gift I ever gave to you. You promised to get me one from that gift shop **do**h. Could you do that today?*

~ Megan

2. *Remember, years ago, you told me you wanted to be a successful musician singing worldwide, and I always dreamed about you being a singer performing in front of a crowd. You always assured me that it was something you'd eventually do but still...*

*If you could choose what will become of me, what would you have wanted me to be? Do gift me something **Re**lated to that.*

~ Megan

3. *Remember our second anniversary when you took **Mi** out to dinner and said it would be a tradition in every one of our anniversaries? Four years have passed without you fulfilling that promise.*

So tonight, I'm reminding you...pick up dinner from our favorite restaurant.

~ Megan

4. Remember the promise we made at Bingo's Diner on the eve of our second anniversary? I have not for once, defaulted.

I bet you've loved every pair of cufflinks I've gotten you.

*I hope you've not forgotten forget-me-nots are my favorite? The florist isn't so **Fa**.*

~ Megan

5. Remember, we always thought going to cinemas was generic, but then when it was a Tom Cruise movie, we just had to see it.

*It was nice. We went, we **So** and I ate your popcorn while you concentrated on the movie. You promised to take your revenge.*

Well, now's your chance. The sequel to that movie is showing soon. This weekend, maybe?

~ Megan

6. Remember my first visit with you to your Mom's? You might not remember what went down that day, but there were statements along the lines of me not knowing 'how to treat a man right'.

Also, do you remember when you promised after your surgery that you'd set things straight with her to her face?

*Cal-**La** today. Tell her she was wrong about me.*

~ Megan

7. Remember how we first met? Valentine's Day and Donuts?

*I don't think I've ever had better-tasting donuts **Ti** ll date.*

Would you get me donuts with my favorite filling from that drive-through?

~ Megan

8. Remember how much you loved music? How we went to numerous concerts and how you sing to me songs you composed for me?

***Do**h that may be long forgotten now, could you write a song just for me, reminding me of the good times we shared?*

~Megan

She had hidden musical motifs within those notes. Do, Re, Mi, Fa, So, La, Ti, Do. Almost as if she was daring me to see them, see her, and see what I had always wanted. My entire life once revolved around music, and Megan loved it. She told me once that I was happiest when I was with the guitar. She had described the way my eyes shone, and my face radiated brilliance. I knew what she was trying to say now. I had to go back to music. *My* music. My hand trembled with this realization that had taken me two weeks of inane requests.

However, there was one final note. Resounding in its finality, crystal clear in repeating to me what she wanted.

Thank you for all the gifts. Now here's one for you.

~ Megan

I saw the divorce papers that were signed already and the keys to the house. There was nothing else I could do. She was gone. I did it to myself. I had pushed her away, and now she was gone.

I walked over to the bedroom and stood in front of the mirror like I did the day she found out about Kelly. But where could she have gone too?

I knew for sure she wouldn't go to her mom. The only place available was Shanice. There was no time to waste. I ran to the sitting room and grabbed my keys from where I had dropped them.

The roads were mercifully free of traffic, which gave me time to think about what I would tell Megan. Again, I should have called her or maybe Shanice, but I didn't know if she wanted to see me. And there was only one way to find out.

I saw her once I arrived. She looked happy and was talking to someone over her shoulder as she stood at the entrance to Shanice's apartment. She was leaving again. Permanently, this time. She must have dropped by to say goodbye to Shanice before she left. I saw her luggage by the door. She went in again without looking back at me. I had to knock.

Breathe, Kevin. Breathe

Oh, wow. Hello, Shanice. Megan...I need to talk to you... just this one last time."

"Well, this is me trying not to miss my flight. I'm almost behind schedule."

I pointed to the car he parked on the street. "I can drive you there, then. All I just want to do is get a chance to talk to...."

She cut me off immediately. I was right. She didn't want to listen to what I had to say. But I had to let her know in any way possible.

"Shanice already offered. It'd be rude to suddenly change plans because you suddenly came along."

I looked past her and right at Shanice, begging her with all my heart without saying anything.

"It's alright. Let Kevin drive you. I'm supposed to put the roast in the oven by bow for tonight. Dinner has to be ready early... it's a school night!"

Yes!

"Alright then. Thank you, but let's speed up. Newark Airport."

"Sure, got it."

I would be able to talk to her in the car. I would have to wait for the right time.

Many thoughts were running through my head. I couldn't find the wherewithal to speak up. She was waiting for me to break the silence, but, at that time, of all times, I had run out of words.

"Um, Megan. We need to talk."

I was caressing the steering wheel, and I could see the airport slowly come into view. I had very little time.

"Yes, you said so earlier," She cut me off.

"I'm sorry. I know I'm flawed and severely lacking... I... mistreated you even though you were only good to me. I'm so sorry I cheated on you."

And I burst into tears. I could feel what she felt when I cheated. At least a fraction of it. My heart was thumping like it was going to stop the very next second.

"You didn't deserve all that bullshit I was serving you. I'm really, really sorry, Megan. I don't know if you'd ever find it in your heart to forgive me."

She just stared at me. I wanted to know what she was thinking, and I wanted to know more than I needed my next breath.

"I don't think I can ever find in anyone else what I found in you. I don't know what pushed me to make all those poor choices, but darling...."

"Megan. Call me Megan."

She was gone. She wasn't my wife anymore. She was divorced. I was divorced. The tears flowed freely now.

"Megan... I know you're still angry, but I can't imagine spending the rest of my life without you being in it. Please, another chance... please."

"Kevin. Let's park for a bit."

I pulled the car over to the side of the road. We couldn't stay long, and I saw her glance at her watch. She wanted to leave, but I would say everything before she left. I composed myself, but the tears wouldn't stop. Who would have thought that two weeks ago, all I wanted was to leave her and run off with Kelly?

I didn't want anything to do with Kelly, and I didn't want anything to do with leaving Megan.

"I was wrong. I was wrong about you, about what I wanted, about my choice of actions... I was wrong, Megan, I admit. But please, let me fix this. I can't risk losing you. I need you; I can't go through life without you by my side, Megan. We've come a long way... We... We can fix this...."

She shook her head.

"Kevin. Kevin, listen to me. It will not work. It did not work then, so why do you think it will now? It's always about you, you, you! Did you stop to consider how I was feeling in the marriage and how I'm feeling now? I was never your priority. Today, you feel like this, but I'm sure after a few days, you'd go back to being your regular self."

She was resolute and firm. There was silence after she said this. There was nothing more I could say as her flight time approached. There was a part of my brain that believed she would listen to me and still wouldn't want to come back, but I had stifled it. Now that part was back and was taunting my futile efforts.

She spoke again.

"Don't beat yourself up, though. Even the best of us make mistakes. Many have, and many will. You got distracted, and you made a hasty decision. Who hasn't? But we all have to live with the consequences of our decisions either way."

There was no reply to that. Every word was correct and absolute. I had to live with the consequences.

"Um, Kevin... my flight is in a few minutes."

I rubbed my face.

"Yeah, that's true. My bad."

I got down from the car and helped her with her luggage, and as she got ready, I realized what was happening. Megan was leaving me forever.

Oh God, Please. Please.

"Please, don't go. Please."

She stared at me for a while, thinking I still had no idea what was going through her head. Then, from nowhere, she hugged me. I put my arms around her back and inhaled that Megan-like scent that I had grown to love for the last time.

"Let's be best friends, Kevin. I'd send you postcards from around the world– or whatever keepsakes people send each other these days," she said.

I couldn't say anything anymore. The tears had clogged my throat, and my mouth was dry, but I held onto her.

"Looks like you have to move the car... And I have to go."

She had to go. She was gone already. I will remember that moment for a very long time.

"Bye."

Epilogue

♥

Megan

Marseilles treated me nicely, and so did Mykonos. It was exhilarating jet-setting all over Europe, meeting new people, and taking the best pictures, both of landscape and consenting people. Going on tours allowed me access to places in Europe I would have only thought existed in fairytales or surreal imaginations.

Was it the stunning views I captured while hiking the Caucasus mountains? Or the dangerous beauty of the cliffs of Moher? I wept when I saw the striking resplendence of Svartifoss. It made me come to terms with my frailty. It was like a refreshing time of self-discovery for me, apart from the pictures I was expected to take of the sights and the plush hospitality centers. I had taken at least a hundred photographs per country and still had Spain to tick off my list.

I have heard from Shanice and the gang. Apparently, Andrea was pregnant now, and Shanice had launched her product line. Candace now also occasionally dropped by the Eirene center, and Tori had now started taekwondo classes. They were doing just great, and that brought me so much joy.

I strolled through the cobblestone streets of Spain, soaking in the sounds, smells, tastes, and sounds. My Spanish was average, but it was still rather obvious I was a foreigner.

I was returning from one of the shoot locations when I saw a roadside soloist who was about to render a number. I was going to walk right past, but something about the first notes he strummed on his guitar struck me as hauntingly familiar.

I paused and listened to the song he was singing. Even the lyrics seemed familiar too.

Rolling in the hay with someone else
Turning with every dip and crest
But you were there watching, tears in your eyes
Heartbeats, constrictions in your chest
I never thought I'd feel this way
You waited, you pushed, and you smiled, my little muse.
The memories we had, the fights, the laughs.
I cherish them, my muse, and I hope this song reaches you.

By the third line, I recognized it as Kevin's song– the one he wrote for me. I was rather surprised it had gained so much traction. *I'm really proud of him. I always thought he was a stellar singer, and now, the world feels so too!*

I walked away, smiling, singing along to the dwindling chorus the singer was belting until he was out of audible range.

I'm in love, and I'm in love
I never left for my heart beats on
I'm in love, oh my love
My little flower, what have I done?
You gave me your all, the best and the worst.
And I threw it all away, and now it burdens like a cross

Except, I wasn't in love anymore, and I had left. For good.

Kevin

I couldn't keep working at that firm with Kelly there, and truth be told, I wasn't very keen about the job. So I left.

I discovered singing on street corners gave me a sense of fulfillment and more joy than I could ever describe. Some of my friends and former colleagues think I'm crazy for quitting my job to take on street and subway singing. You know what? They may be right. *I am crazy. Crazy in love with Megan.*

It's my life's hope and dream that Megan will hear me, consider me, and come back to me. This time I'd do better. I'd do a lot better. I know she's out there, and I hope she knows I'm still waiting for her.

For me, it was a penance of sorts. I had hurt a good woman, and it was only fair I get a recompense. Life is funny, you know. Kelly was not what I thought she was. Chasing after tin foil, I lost true gold, and I will continue to pay for that foolhardy choice for the rest of my life.

It's pretty ironic that on the basis of my life turning into shambles, I became a star. The song I wrote for Megan is now one of the most streamed songs on many platforms. I guess that's just how it was meant to be. I was destined to be a singer who conveyed pain and raw emotions in delicate melodies, but it's rather unfortunate I didn't realize it until now.

Yes, I knew I had a great voice. Those that knew me knew it too. But what we didn't realize was that it lacked genuine emotion, the kind that stemmed from experience. Now, no one can deny that it's there.

As I stood at the street corner of 5th and Main, strumming and singing my heart out, I noticed a dark-haired lady pass behind the crowd.

Megan? She looked back, and I saw that she had a round face, wore glasses, and looked nothing like the woman I had come to love.

I had grown over time to ignore the squealing of the high school girls that tried to get my attention each time I performed. Each time, I scanned the crowd with my eyes, ever coming to a conclusion that:

I have eyes for only one lady, and she isn't here.
Until one day...